A Tramp's Sketches

Stephen Graham

Contents

A TRAMP'S SKETCHES

BY

Stephen Graham

PREFACE

THIS book was written chiefly whilst tramping along the Caucasian and Crimean shores of the Black Sea, and on a pilgrimage with Russian peasants to Jerusalem. Most of it was written in the open air, sitting on logs in the pine forests or on bridges over mountain streams, by the side of my morning fire or on the sea sand after the morning dip. It is not so much a book about Russia as about the tramp. It is the life of the wanderer and seeker, the walking hermit, the rebel against modern conditions and commercialism who has gone out into the wilderness.

I have tramped alone over the battlefields of the Crimea, visited the cemetery where lie so many British dead, wandered along the Black Sea shores a thousand miles to New Athos monastery and Batum, have been with seven thousand peasant pilgrims to Jerusalem, and lived their life in the hospitable Greek monasteries and in the great Russian hostelry at the Holy City, have bathed with them in Jordan where all were dressed in their death-shrouds, and have slept with them a whole night in the Sepulchre.

One cannot make such a journey without great experiences both spiritual and material. On every hand new significances are revealed, both of Russian life and of life itself.

It is with life itself that this volume is concerned. It is personal and friendly, and on that account craves indulgence. Here are the songs and sighs of the wanderer, many lyrical pages, and the very minimum of scientific and topographical matter. It is all written spontaneously and without study, and as such goes forth—all that a seeker could put down of his visions, or could tell of what he sought.

There will follow, if it is given to the author both to write and to publish, a full story of the places he visited along the Black Sea shore, and of the life of the pilgrims on the way to the shrine of the Sepulchre and at the shrine itself. It will be a continuation of the work begun in *Undiscovered Russia.*

Several of these sketches appeared in the *St. James's Gazette,* two in *Country Life,* and one in *Collier's* of New York, being sent out to these papers from the places where they were written. The author thanks the Editors for permission to republish, and for their courtesy in dealing with MSS.

STEPHEN GRAHAM.

I

FAREWELL TO THE TOWN

THE town is one large house of which all the little houses are rooms. The streets are the stairs. Those who live always in the town are never out of doors even if they do take the air in the streets.

When I came into the town I found that in my soul were reflected its blank walls, its interminable stairways, and the shadows of hurrying traffic.

A thousand sights and impressions, unbidden, unwelcome, flooded through the eye-gate of my soul, and a thousand harsh sounds and noises came to me through my ears and echoed within me. I became aware of confused influences of all kinds striving to find some habitation in the temple of my being.

What had been my delight in the country, my receptivity and hospitality of consciousness, became in the town my misery and my despair.

For imagine! Within my own calm mirror a beautiful world had seen itself rebuilded. Mountains and valleys lay within me, robed in sunny and cloudy days or marching in the majesty of storm. I had inbreathed their mystery and outbreathed it again as my own. I had gazed at the wide foaming seas till they had gazed into me, and all their waves waved their proud crests within me. Beauteous plains had tempted, mysterious dark forests lured me, and I had loved them and given them habitation in my being. My soul had been wedded to the great strong sun and it had slumbered under the watchful stars.

The silence of vast lonely places was preserved in my breast. Or against the background of that silence resounded in my being the roar of the billows of the ocean. Great winds roared about my mountains, or the whispering snow hurried over them as over tents. In my valleys I heard the sound of rivulets; in my forests the birds. Choirs of birds sang within my breast. I had been a playfellow with God. God had played with me as with a child.

Bound by so intimate a tie, how terrible to have been betrayed to a town!

For now, fain would the evil city reflect itself in my calm soul, its commerce take up a place within the temple of my being. I had left God's handiwork and come to the manmade town. I had left the inexplicable and come to the realm of the explained. In the holy temple were arcades of shops; through its precincts hurried the trams; the pictures of trade were displayed; men were building hoardings in my soul and posting notices of idol-worship, and hurrying throngs were reading books of the rites of idolatry. Instead of the mighty anthem of the ocean I heard the roar of traffic. Where had been mysterious forests now stood dark chimneys, and the songs of birds were exchanged for the shrill whistle of trains.

And my being began to express itself to itself in terms of commerce.

"Oh God," I cried in my sorrow, "who did play with me among the mountains, refurnish my soul! Purge Thy Temple as Thou didst in Jerusalem of old time, when Thou didst overset the tables of the money-changers."

Then the spirit drove me into the wilderness to my mountains and valleys, by the side of the great sea and by the haunted forests. Once more the vast dome of heaven became the roof of my house, and within the house was rebuilded that which my soul called beautiful. There I refound my God, and my being re-expressed itself to itself in terms of eternal Mysteries. I vowed I should never again belong to the town.

As upon a spring day the face of heaven is hid and a storm descends, winds ruffle the bosom of a pure lake, the flowers droop, wet, the birds cease singing, and rain rushes over all, and then anon the face of heaven clears, the sun shines forth, the flowers look up in tears, the birds sing again, and the pure lake reflects once more the pure depth of the sky, so now my glad soul, which had lost its sun, found it again and remembered its birds and its flowers.

II

NIGHTS OUT ON A PERFECT VAGABONDAGE

I

I HAVE been a whole season in the wilds, tramping or idling on the Black Sea shore, living for whole days together on wild fruit, sleeping for the most part under the stars, bathing every morning and evening in the clear warm sea. It is difficult to tell the riches of the life I have had, the significance of the experience. I have felt pulse in my veins wild blood which my instincts had forgotten in the town. I have felt myself come back to Nature.

During the first month after my departure from the town I slept but thrice under man's roof. I slept all alone, on the hillside, in the maize-fields, in the forest, in old deserted houses, in caves, ruins, like a wild animal gone far afield in search of prey. I never knew in advance where I should make my night couch; for I was Nature's guest and my hostess kept her little secrets. Each night a new secret was opened, and in the secret lay some pleasant mystery. Some of the mysteries I guessed—there are many guesses in these pages—some I only tried to guess, and others I could only wonder over. All manner of mysterious things happen to us in sleep; the sick man is made well, the desperate hopeful, the dull man happy. These things happen in houses which are barred and shuttered and bolted. The power of the Night penetrates even into the luxurious apartments of kings, even into the cellars of the slums. But if it is potent in these, how much more is it potent in its free unrestricted domain, the open country. He who sleeps under the stars is bathed in the elemental forces which in houses only creep to us through keyholes. I may say from experience that he who has slept out of doors every day for a month, nay even for a week, is at the end of that time a new man. He has entered into new relationship with the world in which he lives, and has allowed the gentle creative hands of Nature to re-shape his soul.

The first of my nights after leaving the town was spent on a shaggy grass patch on a cliff, under three old twisted yew trees. Underfoot was an abundance of wild lavender and the air was laden with the scent. I am now at New Athos monastery, ten miles from Sukhum, and am writing this in the cell that the hospitable monks have given me. My last night was in a deep cavern at the base of a high rock on a desert shore.

The first night was warm and gentle, though it was followed by several that were stormy. Wrapped in my rug I felt not a shiver of cold, even at dawn. As I lay at my ease, I looked out over the far southern sea sinking to sleep in the dusk. The glistening and sparkling of the water passed away—the sea became a great bale of grey-blue silk, soft, smooth, dreamy, like the garment of a sorceress queen.

I slipped into sleep and slipped out again as easily as one goes from one room to another, sometimes sleeping one hour or half an hour at a time, or more often one moment asleep, one moment awake, like the movement of a boat on the waves.

Once when I wakened, I started at an unforeseen phenomenon. The moon in her youth was riding over the sea as bright as it is possible to be, and down below her she wrote upon the waves and expressed herself in new variety, a long splash of lemon-coloured light over the placid ocean, a dream picture, something of magic.

It was a marvellous sight, something of that which is indicated in pictures, but which one cannot recognise as belonging to the world of truth—something impressionistic. To waken to see something so beautiful is to waken for the first time, it is verily to be in part born; for therein the soul becomes aware of something it had not previously imagined: looking into the mirror of Nature, it sees itself anew.

Where my sleeping-place would be had been a secret, and this was the mystery in it, the further secret. I was definitely aware even on my first night out that I had entered a new world.

To sleep, to wake and find the moon still dreaming, to see the moon's dream in the water, to sleep again and wake, so—till the dawn. Such was my night under the old yews, the first spent with these southern stars on a long vagabondage.

II

How different was last night, how full of weariness after heavy tramping through leagues of loose stones. I had been tramping from desolate Cape Pitsoonda over miles and miles of sea holly and scrub through a district where were no people. I had been living on crab-apples and sugar the whole day, for I could get no provisions. It is a comic diet. I should have liked to climb up inland to find a resting-place and seek out houses, but I was committed to the seashore, for the cliffs were sheer, and where the rivers made what might have been a passage, the forest tangles were so barbed that they would tear the clothes off one's back. In many places the sea washed the cliffs and I had to undress in order to get past. It was with resignation that I gave up my day's tramping and sought refuge for the night in a deep and shapely cavern.

There was plenty of dry clean sand on the floor, and there was a natural rock pillow. I spread out my blanket and lay at length, looking out to the sea. I lay so near the waves that at high tide I could have touched the foam with my staff. I watched the sun go down and felt pleased that I had given up my quest of houses and food until the morrow. As I lay so leisurely watching the sun, it occurred to me that there was no reason why man should not give up quests when he wanted to—he was not fixed in a definite course like the sun.

Sunset was beautiful, and dark-winged gulls continually alighted on the glowing waves, alighted and swam and flew again till the night. Then the moon lightened up the sea with silver, and all night long the waves rolled and rolled again, and broke and splashed and lapped. The deep cavern was filled with singing sounds that at first frightened me, but at last lulled me to sleep as if a nurse had sung them.

III

Between these two beds what a glorious Night picture-book, a book telling almost entirely of the doings of the moon. I remember how I slept once under a wild walnut-tree. In front of me rose to heaven forested hills, and the night clothed them in majesty. Presently the moon came gently from her apartments and put out a slender hand, grasped the tree-tops, and pulled herself up over the world. She showed herself to me in all her glory, and then in a minute was gone again; for she entered into a many-windowed cloud castle and roamed from room to room. As she passed from window to window I knew by the light where she was. A calm night. The moon went right across the sky and returned to her home. Rain came before the dawn, and then mists crept down over the forests and hid them from my view. Cold, cold! The mountains were hidden by a cloud. Loose stones rolled down a cliff continually and a wind sighed. I snuggled myself into my blanket and waited for an hour. Then the sun gained possession of the sky.

I went down to the river, gathered sticks—they were very damp—and made a fire. Once the fire began to burn it soon increased in size, for I had gathered a great pile of little twigs and they soon dried and burned. Then in their burning they dried bigger twigs, sticks, cudgels, logs. I boiled my kettle and made tea.

Whilst I bathed in the river the sun gave a vision of his splendour: a thousand mists trembled at his gaze. An hour later it was a very hot day, and the village folk coming out of their houses could scarcely have dreamed how reluctantly the night had retired at the dawn—with what cold and damp the morning had begun.

IV

Another night, just after moonrise, a wind arose and drove in front of it the whole night - long a great thunderstorm, with lightnings and rollings and grumblings and mutterings, but never a spot of rain. At dawn, when I looked out to sea I saw the whole dreadful array of the storm standing to leeward like ships that had passed in the night, and as though baulked in pursuit the roll of the thunder came across the sky sullenly, though with a note of defeat

The nights were often cold and wet, and it became necessary for me to make my couch under bridges or in caves or holes of the earth. On the skirts of the tobacco plantations and in the swampy malarial region where the ground never gets dry I slept beside bonfires. I learned of the natives to safeguard against fever by placing withered leaves on bark or wilted bracken leaves between myself and the ground. At a little settlement called Olginka I slept on an accumulation of logs outside the village church. On this occasion I wrapped myself up in all the clothes I possessed, and so saved myself from the damp. Next morning, however, my blanket was so wet with dew that I could wring it, though I had felt warm all night. I had always to guard against the possibility of rain, and I generally made my couch in pleasant proximity to some place of shelter—a bridge, a cave, or a house; and more than once I had to abandon my grass bed in the very depth of the night, and take up the alternative one in shelter.

V

A tremendous thunderstorm took place about a fortnight after I left home. I had built a stick fire and was making tea for myself at the end of a long cloudless summer day, and taking no care, when suddenly I looked up to the sky and saw the evening turning swiftly to night before my eyes. The sun was not due to set, but the western horizon seemed as it were to have risen and gone forth to meet it. A great black bank of cloud had come up out of the west and hidden away the sun before his time.

I hastened to put my tea things into my pack and take to the road, for it was necessary to find a convenient night place. In a quarter of an hour it was night. At regular intervals all along the road were the brightly lit lamps of glow-worms; they looked like miniature street lights, the fitting illumination of a road mostly occupied by hedgehogs.

I found a dry resting-place under a tree and laid myself out to sleep, watching the moon who had just risen perfectly, out of the East; but I had hardly settled myself when I was surprised by a gleam of lightning. Turning to the west, I saw the vast array of cloud that had overtaken the sun, coming forward into the night—eclipsing the sky.

A storm? Would it reach me? My wishes prompted comforting answers and I lay and stared at the sky, trying to find reassurance. I did not feel inclined to stir, but the clouds came on ominously. I marked out a bourne across the wide sky and resolved that if the shadow crept past certain bright planets in the north, south, and centre, I would take it as a sign, repack my wraps, and seek shelter in a farm-house. But the clouds came on and on. Slowly but surely the great army advanced and the lightnings became more frequent. My sky-line was passed. I rose sorrowfully, put all my things in the knapsack, and took the road once again.

The lightning rushed past on the road and, blazing over the forests, lit up the wide night all around. Overhead the sky was cut across: in the east was a perfectly clear sky except at the horizon where the moon seemed to have left behind fiery vapours; in the west and overhead lay the dense black mass of the storm cloud. The clouds came forward in regular array like an army. Nothing could hold them back;

they came on—appallingly. And the moon looked at the steady advance and her light gleamed upon the front ranks as if she were lighting them with many lanterns.

I had lain down to sleep quite sober-hearted, but now as the lightnings played around I began to feel as excited as if I were in a theatre—my blood burned. I had tired feet, but I forgot them. I walked swiftly. I felt ready to run, to dance. Very strangely there was at the same time a presentiment that I might be struck by lightning. But all Nature was madly excited with me and also shared my presentiment of destruction. We lived together like the victim and the accomplices in a Dionysian sacrifice and orgy.

And the clouds kept on gaining! Far away I heard the storm wind and the clamour of the sea. The thunder moaned and sobbed. I hurried along the deserted road and asked my heart for a village, a house, a church, a cave, anything to shield from the oncoming drench.

Spying a light far away on a hill, I left the road and plunged towards it. I went over many maize-fields, by narrow paths through the tall waving grain, the lightning playing like firelight among the sheath-like leaves. I crossed a wide tobacco plantation and approached the light on the hill, by a long, heavily-rutted cart-track. This led right up to the doors of a farmhouse. Big surly dogs came rushing out at me, but I clumped them off with my stick, and having much doubt in my mind as to the sort of reception I should get, I knocked at the windows and doors. I expected to be met by a man with a gun, for the dogs had made such a rumpus that any one might have been alarmed.

The door was opened by a tall Russian peasant.

"May I spend the night here?" I asked.

The man smiled and put out his arms as if to embrace me.

"Yes, of course. Why ask? Come inside," he replied.

"I thought of sleeping in the open air," I added, "but the storm coming up I saw I should be drenched."

"Why sleep outside when man is ready to receive you?" said the peasant. "It is unkind to pass our houses by. Why do you deny your brothers so? You said you slept in the fields, eh? That is bad. You shouldn't. The earth here is full of evil, and the malaria comes up with the dampness. Your bones grow brittle and break, or they go all soft, you shrivel up and become white, or swellings come out on you and you get bigger and bigger until you die. No, no! God be thanked you came to me."

He asked me would I sleep in the house or on the maize straw. His sons slept on the maize; it was covered, and so, sheltered from the rain. I could sleep in the house if I liked, but it was more comfortable on the straw. His three sons slept there, but as it was a festival they had not come home yet.

I agreed to the straw. My host led me to a sort of large open barn, a barn without walls, a seven-feet depth of hay and straw surmounted by a high roof on poles.

"If you feel cold, or if the rain comes in, just burrow down under the straw," said the peasant. "Very glad I am that you have come to me, that you have done me the honour. Much better to ask hospitality than to sleep out."

I quite agreed it was much better to sleep with man on such a night. The lightnings were now all about—never leaving a second's pure darkness. The thunder grew more powerful and rolled forward from three sides.

My host stood by me after I had lain down, a whole hour. He was most hilarious, having partaken plentifully of festival fare. He warned me repeatedly against sleeping on the ground, and advised me to find bark or withered branches to lie upon if I would not seek shelter with man. The increasing storm did not seem to impress him in the slightest. He was all agog to tell me his family history and to compare the state of agriculture in England with that in Russia. Only when his sons came home and the heavy rain spots had begun to shower down upon him did he finally shake my hand, wish me well, cross himself, and stump off back to the house.

Three tall young men scrambled over me into the straw and buried themselves: two laughed and talked, the other was silent and frightened. There was no sleep. The thunder grew louder and louder, and the lightning rushed over our faces like the sudden glare of a searchlight. All four of us put our faces to the straw to shut out the light, and we tried to sleep. But we knew that the tempest at its worst had yet to break. Suddenly came a sharp premonitory crash just above us, near, astonishing. One of the young men, who had just dozed off, woke up and scratched his head, saying—

"The little bear has got into the maize. Eh, brothers, this is going to be a big piece of work."

Then a great wind broke out of the sky and tore through the forests like armies of wild beasts. The trees within our view bent down as if they would break in two; the moon above them was overswept by the cloud. When the moon's light had gone the night became darker and the lightning brighter. The framework of our shelter rocked to and fro in the gale and we felt as if upon the sea; the straw and the hay jumped up as if alive, and great lumps of thatch were rent out of the roof, showing the sky and letting in the rain. I looked for the ruin of our shelter.

But the hurricane passed on. The rain came in its place. The great forty-day flood re-accomplished itself in an hour. We heard the beat of the rain on the earth: in ten minutes it was the hiss of the rain on the flooded meadows. By the sulphurous illuminations we saw almost continuously the close-packed, drenching rain. . . . The wet came in. We burrowed deep down into the straw and slept like some new sort of animal.

VI

On other nights heavy rain came on unexpectedly, and I discovered how pleasant a bed may be made just under the framework of a bridge. The bridge is a favourite resort of the Russian tramp and pilgrim, and I have often come across their comfortable hay or bracken beds there. Indeed I seldom go across a bridge at night without thinking there may be some such as myself beneath it.

When the weather is wet it is much more profitable to sleep in a village—there is hospitality there, and the peasant wife gives you hot soup and dries your clothes. But often villages are far apart, and when you are tramping through the forest there may be twenty miles without a human shelter. I remember I found empty houses, and though I used them they were most fearsome. I had more thrills in them than in the most lonely resting-places in the open. Some distance from Gagri I found an old ruined dwelling, floorless, almost roofless, but still affording shelter. I had many misgivings as I lay there. Was the house haunted? Was it some one else's shelter? Had some family lived there and all died out? You may imagine the questions that assailed me, once I had lain down. But whether evil was connected with the house or no, it was innocuous for me. Nothing happened; only the moon looked through the open doorway; winds wandered among the broken rafters, and far away owls shrieked.

Again, on the way to Otchemchiri I came upon a beautiful cottage in the forest and went to ask hospitality, but found no one there. The front door was bolted but the back door was open. I walked in and took a seat. As there were red-hot embers in the fire some one had lately been there, and would no doubt come back—so I thought. But no one came: twilight grew to night in loneliness and I lay down on the long sleeping bench and slept. It was like the house of the three bears but that there was no hot porridge on the table. But no bears came; only next morning I was confronted by a half-dressed savage, a veritable Caliban by appearance but quite harmless, an idiot and deaf and dumb. I made signs to him and he went out and brought in wood, and we remade the fire together.

I have slept out in many places—in England, in the Caucasus where it was amongst the most lawless people in Europe, in North Russian forests where the bear is something to be reckoned with—but I have never come to harm. The most glorious and wonderful nights I ever had were almost sleepless ones, spent looking at the stars and tasting the new sensations. Yet even in respect of rest it seems to me I have thriven better out of doors. There is a real tranquillity on a mountain side after the sun has gone down, and a silence, even though the crickets whistle and owls cry, though the wind murmurs in the trees above or the waves on the shore below. The noises in houses are often intolerable and one has to wait till every noise in the house and in the street has died away. It is marvellous how easily one recuperates in the open air. Even the cold untires and refreshes. Then, even if one lies awake, the night passes with extraordinary rapidity. It is always a marvel to me how long the day seems by comparison with the night when I sleep out of doors. A sleepless night in a house is an eternity, but it is only a brief interlude under the stars. I believe the animal creation that sleeps in the field is so in harmony with nature and so unself-conscious that night does not seem more than a quarter of an hour and a little cloudy weather. Perhaps the butterflies do not even realise that night endures; darkness comes—they sleep; darkness flees—they wake again. I think they have no dreams.

VII

It is peculiar, the tramp's feeling about night. When the sun goes down he begins to have an awkward feeling, a sort of shame; he wants to hide himself, to put his head somewhere out of sight. He finds his night place, and even begins to fall asleep as he arranges it. He feels heavy, dull. The thoughts that were bright and shapely by day become dark and ill-proportioned like shadows. He tosses a while, and stares at the stars. At last the stars stare at him; his eyes close; he sleeps. Three hours pass—it is always a critical time, three hours after sunset; many sleeping things stir at that time. His thoughts are bright for a moment, but then fall heavy again. He wonders at the moon, and the moon wonders. She is hunting on a dark mountain side.

The next sleep is a long one, a deep one, and ghosts may pass over the sleeper, imps dance on his head, rats nibble at his provisions; he wakes not. He is under a charm—nought of evil can affect him, for he has prayed. Encompassed with dangers, the tramp always prays "Our Father," and that he may be kept for the one who loves him. Prayers are strong out of doors at night, for they are made at heaven's gate in the presence of the stars.

An hour before dawn a new awakening. Oh dear, night not gone! The tramp is vexed. The moon has finished her hunting, and is going out of the night with her dark huntsmen; she passes through the gate. Peerless hunter!

The sky is full of light, a sort of dull, paper-lantern light. In an hour it will be morning. The side on which I have been lying is sore. I turn over and reflect joyfully that when next I wake it will be day. Moths are flitting in the dawn twilight: yes, in an hour it will be day.

Ah, ha, ha! The sleeper yawns and looks up. There is blue in the clouds, pale blue like that of a baby's eyes. A cart lumbers along the road, the first cart of the morning. I reflect that if I remain where I am people may come and look at me. Ten minutes hesitation, and then suddenly I make up my mind and rise.

I feel a miserable creature, a despicable sort of person, one who has lately been beaten, a beggar who has just been refused alms. In the half-light of dawn it seems I scarcely have a right to exist. Or I feel a sort of self-pity. How often have I said as I gathered up my stiff limbs and damp belongings in the mist of the morning, "And the poor old tramp lifts himself and takes to the road once more, trudge, trudge, trudge—a weary life!"

The mansion of my soul has been housing phantoms all the night. They may not stay after sunrise; they look out of my face with bleared eyes. It is they who gibber and chatter thus at dawn, leaving me with no more self-assurance than a man on ticket-of-leave.

But as the sun comes up, behold the spirits evaporate, the films pass away from my eyes, and I am lighter, blither, happier, stronger. Then in my heart birds begin to sing in chorus. I am myself once more.

A fire, a kettle, and while the kettle boils, into the sea, giving my limbs to the sparkling buoyant water. Then am I super-self, if such an expression may be permitted. So passes the vagabond's night.

Thus somehow one comes into new harmony with Nature, and the personal rhythm enters into connection with all things that sleep and wake under the stars. One lives a new life. It is something like the change from bachelor to married life. You are richer and stronger. When you move some one else moves with you, and that was unexpected. Whilst you live Nature lives with you.

I have written of the night, for the night hallows the day, and the day does not hallow the night except for those who toil.

III

THE LORD'S PRAYER

THE Lord's Prayer is a very intimate whispering of the soul with God. It is also the perfect child's prayer, and the tramp being much of a child, it is his.

Many people have their private interpretations of the prayer, and I have heard preachers examine it clause by clause. It can mean many things. It must mean different things to people of different lives. It is something very precious to the tramp.

The tramp is the lonely one: walking along all by himself all day by the side of the sounding waves he is desolated by loneliness, and when he lies down at dusk all alone he feels the need of loving human friends. But his friends are far away.

He becomes once more a little trusting child, one who, though he fears, looks up to the face of a great strong Father. He feels himself encompassed about by dangers: perhaps some one watched him as he smoothed out his bracken bed; or if he went into a cave a robber saw him and will come later in the night, when he is fast asleep, murder him, and throw his body into the sea; or he may have made his bed in the path of the bear or in the haunt of snakes. Many, many are the shapes of terror that assail the mind of the wanderer. How good to be a little boy who can trust in a great strong Father to "deliver him from evil"!

And each clause of that lovely prayer has its special reality. Thus "Give us this day our daily bread" causes him to think, not so much of getting wages on the morrow as of the kindly fruits of the earth that lie in the trees and bushes like anonymous gifts, and of the hospitality of man.

Most beautiful of all to the tramp is the wish—"Thy Kingdom come—Thy Will be done in earth as it is in heaven." For it is thus understood: Thy Will be done in earth—I am that earth. "Thy Kingdom come" means Thy Kingdom come in me—may my soul lie like a pure mirror before the beauty of the world, may the beauty of the world be reflected in me till the whole beautiful world is my heart. Then shall my heart be pure, and that which I see will be God. Thy Will be done in me as it is done in heaven.

And the tramp asks himself as he lies full length on the earth and looks up at the stars—are you a yea-sayer? Do you say "Yes" to life? Do you raise your face in wonder to the beauty of the world? Do you stand with bare feet in sacred places? Do you remember always the mystery and wonder that is in your fellow-man whom you meet upon the road? . . . "Hallowed be Thy Name."

Does the wanderer love all things? It is a condition of all things loving him. He must have perfect peace in his heart for the kingdom to be built there. . . . "Forgive us our trespasses."

We may be tempted to forget Thee, may fear danger and our hearts be ruffled, may be tempted to forget that our fellow-man is one like ourselves, with our mystery and wonder, and having a very loving human heart either apparent or prevented. We may be tempted to forget the mystery of our own souls. The tramp prays to be led not into such temptation. For, with the Father above him, is the power, the kingdom, and the glory, for ever and ever.

As I said, prayers are strong out of doors, made in the presence of all the stars. One is compassed about with a great cloud of witnesses. There is calm all around and in one's own heart. The mysterious beauty of the starry sky reflects itself in the soul, and across its mirror sails the pale moon. My own body becomes a cradle in which the little Christ Child sleeps. There are angels everywhere. I am in universal keeping, for the stars are all looking and pointing to me. Because of the little Child the shepherds near by hear heavenly harmony, and journeying through the night to the land of dreams come the three wonderful old kings with gifts.

IV

DAYS

IT is because I have been tempered by the coldness of the night that I am not overwhelmed by the heat of the day. Because the night is dark and cool and sweet I see the true colours of the day, and the noon sun does not dazzle me. The tramp's eyes open and then they open again: at midday his eyes are wider than those of indoor folk. He is nearer to the birds because he has slept with them in the bush. They also are nearer to him, for the night has left her mysterious traces upon his face and garments, something which humans cannot see, not even the tramp himself, but which the wild things recognise right enough.

The tramp walks. His road is one that may only be walked upon. People on wheels are never on it: at least, I never met a wheel person who had seen on either side of the road what the tramp sees—and a road is not only a path, but that which is about it. The wheel is the great enemy of Nature, whether it be the wheel of a machine or of a vehicle. Nature abhors wheels. She will not be wooed by cyclists, motorists, goggled motor-cyclists, and the rest: she is not like a modern young lady who, despite ideals, *must* marry, and will take men as they are found in her day and generation.

The woman of the woods who dresses herself in flowers, and whose voice is as birds' songs, is the same yesterday, to-day, and tomorrow—not new-fangled. You must go to her; she will not come to you. You must live as she does.

Therefore the tramp moves *naturally,* on his feet. He comes into step. And sleeping out of doors, living in the sun, eating forest berries, washing in the stream or in the sea, all these are part of a coming into step.

How this *coming back* develops the temperament! I left the town timid, almost a townsman, expecting not only the dangers that were but also all those that were not. I half believed all the tales by which stay-at-home people tried to warn or frighten me. Though taking the road with every aspect of carelessness and boldness, I confessed to my heart that I was a coward. Then came my first week's tramping, and I emerged a different man. I felt bold. A few days later still I nursed a stick in my hand, saying, "If a robber comes, let him come! We'll have a struggle." Leaving the town I scanned the faces of the passers-by apprehensively, and said "Good-morning" or "Good-evening" very meekly to all dangerous-looking persons, but a fortnight later I was even strutting on the road with a smile almost malicious on my lips.

I felt myself growing wilder. The truth broke upon me in an introspective moment one morning as I was nearing Sotchi. I felt I had changed. I stopped to take stock of my new life and ways. I had been living in the forest and on the seashore, away from mankind, on Nature's gifts. All my days from dawn to sunset I hunted for food. My life was food-hunting. I certainly wrote not a line and thought less. In my mind formed only such elementary ideas as "Soon more grapes," "These berries are not the best," "More walnuts," "Oh, a spring; I must drink there."

Something from the ancient past was awakened. I saw a bunch of wild grapes, my heart leapt, and without a thought I jumped to it and took it. Or I saw a fresh trickling stream pouring over the ledges of the rocks, and I rushed and pressed my lips to the bubbling water. There was no intermediary between Nature's gifts and the man who needed them. Wish was translated into act without the aid of thought.

One day I was lost in the forest among the giant tangles and I was not at all anxious to find the way out again. Perhaps I might have lived there all the Autumn, and only when the berries and nuts were exhausted and the cold winter winds sought me out should I come skulking back to the haunts of men like some wild animal made tame by Winter.

I was aware, therefore, of a new experience, a modification in personality, a change of rhythm. I was walking with Nature, marching with her, with all her captains the great trees and her infantry the little bushes, and I caught in my ears her marching music. I was thrilled by the common chord that makes crowds act as one man, that in this case made my heart beat in unison with all the wild things. I may as well say at once I love them all and am ready to live with them and for them.

V

THE QUESTION OF THE SCEPTIC

"THAT'S all very well, but don't you often get bored?" asked a sceptic. "I enjoy a weekend in the country, or a good Sunday tramp in Richmond Park or Epping Forest. I take my month on the Yorkshire moors with pleasure, or I spend a season in Switzerland or Spain, and I don't mind sleeping under a bush and eating whatever I can get in shepherds' cottages. I can well appreciate the simple life and the country life, but I'm perfectly sure I should pine away if I had to live it always. I couldn't stand it. I'd rather be debarred from the country altogether than not go back to town. The town is much more indispensable to me. I feel the country life is very good in so far as it makes one stronger and fitter to work in town again, but as an end in itself it would be intolerable."

This was a question I needed to answer not only to the sceptic but to myself. It is true the wanderer often feels bored, even in beautiful places. I am bored some days every year, no matter where I spend them, and I shall always be. I get tired of this world and want another. That is a common feeling, if not often analysed.

There is, however, another boredom, that of the weariness of the body, or its satiety of country air; the longing for the pleasures of the town, the tides of the soul attracted by the moon of habit. The tramp also confesses to that boredom. But when he gets back to the town to enjoy it for a while he swiftly finds it much more boring than the country.

If every one went to the country and lived the simple life when he was inclined, the size of European towns would be diminished to very small proportions. The evil of a town is that it establishes a tyranny and keeps its people against the people's true desires.

I said to my sceptical friend: "Those who praise the simple life and those who scoff at it are both very extravagant as a rule. Let the matter be stated temperately. The tramp does not want a world of tramps—that would never do. The tramps— better call them the rebels against modern life—are perhaps only the first searchers for new life. They know themselves as necessarily only a few, the pioneers. Let the townsman give the simple life its place. Every one will benefit by a little more simplicity, and a little more living in communion with Nature, a little more of the country. I say, 'Come to Nature altogether,' but I am necessarily misunderstood by those who feel quickly bored. Good advice for all people is this—live the simple life as much as you can *till you're bored.* Some people are soon bored: others never are. Whoever has known Nature once and loved her will return again to her. Love to her becomes more and more."

But whoever has resolved the common illusions of the meaning of life, and has seen even in glimpses the naked mystery of our being, finds that he absolutely must live in the world which is outside city walls. He wants to explore this desert island in space, and with it to explore the unending significance of his deathless spirit.

VI

A THING OF BEAUTY IS A JOY FOR EVER

ROSTOF on the Don is always beautiful when one leaves it to go south. Nothing can efface from my mind the picture of it as I saw it when first going to the Caucasus. The sunset illumined it with the hues of romance. All the multiplicity of its dingy buildings shone as if lit up from within, and their dank and mouldy greens and blues and yellows became burning living colours. The town lay spread out upon the high banks of the Don and every segment of it was crowned with a church. The gilt domes blazed in the sunlight and the crosses above them were changed into pure fire. Round about the town stretched the grey-green steppe, freshened by the river-side, but burned down to the suffering earth itself on the horizon. Then over all, like God's mercy harmonising man's sins, the effulgence of a light-blue southern sky.

By that scene I have understood the poet's thought—

To draw one beauty into the heart's core
And keep it changeless.

Yet how transient is the appearance of beauty. It has an eternity not in itself but in the heart. Thus I look out at the ever-changing ocean and suddenly, involuntarily ejaculate, "How beautiful!" yet before I can call another to witness the scene it has changed. Only in the heart the beauty is preserved. Thus we see a woman in her youth and beauty, and then in a few years look again and find her worn and old. The beauty has passed away; its eternity is in the heart.

We have a choice, to live in the shadow and shine of the outer life where visions fade, or to live with all the beauty we have ever known, where it is treasured, in the heart. Choosing the former we at last perish with the world, but choosing the latter we ourselves receive an immortality in the here and now. The one who chooses the latter shall never grow old, and the beauty of his world can never pass away.

Nietzsche could not tolerate the doctrine of the "immaculate perception" of Beauty. To him Beauty was ***une promesse de bonheur;*** Beauty was a lure and a temptation, it had no virtue in itself, but its value lay in the service rendered to the ulterior aims of Nature. Thus the beauty hung in woman's face was a device of the Life-force for the continuance of the race; strange beauty lured men to strange ends, and one of these ends the German philosopher divined and named as the Superman. Even the beauty of Nature was merely a temptation of man's will. The Kantian conception of the disinterested contemplation of Beauty Nietzsche likened to the moon looking at the earth at night and giving the earth only dreams; but the Stendhalian conception of Beauty as a promise of happiness he likened to the sun looking at the earth and causing her to bear fruit.

Darwin as much as said, "Beauty has been the gleam which the instinct of the race has followed in its upward development. Beauty has been the genius of Evolution." Thus science has lent its authority to philosophy. The idea is charming. In its power it is irresistible. It certainly dominates modern literary art, being the principal dynamic of Ibsen and Bernard Shaw and all their followers.

It is a very important matter. There can be nothing more important in literary art, and indeed in one's articulate conception of the meaning of life, than the notion of what is beautiful. What if this conception be narrow, what if it be simply a generalisation, a generalisation from too few observations? What if the wish were father to the thought?

The only test of philosophy and art is experience. And it is the wanderer, the life-explorer without irrelevant preoccupations, who is the true naturalist, collecting experiences and making maps for spiritual eyes. What then does the wanderer note?

First, that the knowledge of the beautiful is an affirmation. Something in the soul suddenly rises up and ejaculates "Yes" to some outside phenomenon, and then he is aware that he is looking at Beauty. As he gazes he knows himself in communion with what he sees—sometimes that communion is a great joy and sometimes a great sadness. Thus, looking at the opening of dawn he is filled with gladness, his spirits rising with the sun; he wishes to shout and to sing. He is one with the birds that have begun singing and with all wild Nature waking refreshed after the night. But looking out at evening of the same day over the grey sea he is filled with unutterable sorrow.

I remember how all night long in the North region, where the light does not leave the sky, I looked out at the strange beauty of the white night and felt all the desolateness of the world, all the exiledom of man upon it. There was no lure, no temptation in that. The Æolian harp of the heart does not always discourse battle music, and on this night it was as if an old sad minstrel sat before me and played unendingly one plaint, the story of a lost throne, of a lost family, lost children, a lost world. Thus a thought came to me: "We are all the children of kings; on our spiritual bodies are royal seals. Sometime or other we were abandoned on this beautiful garden, the world. We expected some one to return for us; but no one came. We lived on, and to forget homesickness devised means of pleasure, diversions, occupations, games. Some have entirely forgotten the lost heritage and the mystery of their abandonment; their games absorbed them, they have become gamblers, they have theories of chance, their talk is all of Progress of one sort or another. They forget the great mystery of life. We tramps and wanderers remember. It is our religion to remember, to count nothing as important beside the initial mystery. For us it is sweeter to remember than to forget. The towns would always have us forget, but in the country we always remember again. What is beautiful is every little rite that reminds us of our mysteries."

This is a most persistent experience, and Beauty thereby promises us happiness, but in a strange way seems to tell of happiness past. It lures not forward unless to the exploration of the "prison-house" once more.

Even the beauty of woman is not always a lure. There is a beauty in woman which makes one glad, but there is the beauty that haunts one like a great sadness, besides the beauty that draws one nearer to her. There is the seductive beauty of Cleopatra, but there is also the almost repulsive beauty of Medea, and besides both there is the mysterious beauty of Helen or of Eve.

Beauty is also a great possession, and that is another conception, another mystery. We lie like a mirror in the presence of Beauty, and it builds the very temple of our souls. Beauty is the gold of earthly experience. It is essentially that which in looking round our eyes like best, that which they say swiftly "Yes" to. We enter into communion with the beautiful as with a beloved object. We make it part of ourselves. We absorb it into that which is integral and immortal—our very essence. "A thing of beauty is a joy for ever: its loveliness can never pass away "is a truth of experience, not the idle fancy of the poet. For to have seen the beautiful is not inconsequential, it is not even a responsibility entirely your own; the beautiful thing has also seen you. Henceforth your life can never be quite the same, and the beautiful thing looked upon has either become less or more beautiful.

VII

A STILL-CREATION-DAY

THE blue-green sea is living velvet, and full of light-rings; it goes out to a distant mauve horizon, near which sea-gulls with white gleaming wings are flying. Many gulls are fluttering on the red buoys in the water.

It is late in a December afternoon on the south coast of the Crimea. It is Yalta, beloved of all Russians, and I have come tramping to it—which Russians never do—and I am intending to spend lazy days looking with the gay town and all its white villas at the glorious spectacle of the southern sea. All the rest of Russia is gripped by winter, but here there is sanctuary and forgiveness. I have been tramping on the cold, cold steppes, frozen, forced to get back into myself and hide like the trees, and when I came here it seemed somehow as if Nature herself had been angry with me, relented, and was now showing me all her tenderness again. All along the road I found violets in the little bushes, and I wore them as a forgiveness gift from a woman that I love.

When a woman smiles upon a man she bids him live, and when she frowns he can but die. To-day the woman of all women has smiled on me, Nature herself.

Along the road I had that pleasant life with myself that one has the day after one's birthday, when one has kept good resolutions two days. My old self carried, as it were, within me a little child, and the child chattered and lisped to me.

Delightful tramping along a road high over the shore! Below me, stretching far to East and to West, blue and glorious like summer, was the immense sea, all in dazzling radiance under the noonday sun. A bank of grey-blue mist lay over the South, and marked the domain where winter was felt. Up above me stood great grey rocks, stained here and there the colour of rose porphyry. The tops of these rocks, even here as I look up at them from Yalta, are outlined with a bright white line—winter and hoar-frost hold sway there also.

I have been in the sight of nut-brown hillsides, something absolutely perfect, the warm living colour of thousands of little, closely packed French oak trees, all withered, and holding still their little withered leaves. The colour of these hills was the colour of Nature's eyes.

There was silence too—such wonderful silence, one could hear one's own heart beating. Such a morning was indeed what Richter calls a "still-creation-day," that still silence of the heart that prefaces new revelation, as the brooding of the dove on the waters the creation of a world. You must know I saw the dawn, and have been with the sun all day. I slept at a Greek coffee-house, but was up whilst the sky was yet dark and the waves all cloudy purple. There was just one gleam of light in the dark sky, just one little promise. The great cliffs were all in their night cloaks, and night shapes were on the road. All Nature was in the night world, and I felt as if I were continuing my last night's tramping, and not starting upon a new day. Yet in the night of my heart was also just that one gleam of whiteness in the East, one little promise. I knew the whiteness must get more and more, and the darkness less and less. I stood on the cliff road and watched the waves become all alive, playing with their shadows as the light diffused in the sky, and the white lines of the East turned to rosy ribbons. Then the dawn twilight came and the night shapes slunk away. The Tartars and Greeks took down their shutters in the little village hard by.

The sea became green, the rocks all grey, and then, as I watched, the rim of the sun rose over the horizon and the sea held it as a scimitar of fire. The white disc rose, a miracle; it looked very large, as if it had grown bigger in the night. It paused a moment in the sea and then suddenly seemed to bound up from it: it flooded the world with light. Then, as if from his hands angels were leaping, thousands of gulls were descried on the sea, their gleaming wings seeming to be the very meaning of morning. Out of the sea under the dawn, dark dolphins came leaping toward the shore. The sea became a grey expanse over which the sun made a silver roadway. There commenced the quiet, quiet morning, and the still-creation-day.

Now the day is ending, and the sun goes down behind the hills at Yalta, the mist bank over the southern horizon catches the reflection of true sunset tints, and transmits them to the velvety water, full of light-rings. I have been sitting on a pleasure seat on the sand all the afternoon, and now I go to the end of the long pier. There one may see another vision of the mystery of the day, for the sea-waves are full of living autumn colours, of luminous withered leaves and faded rose petals; they are still living velvet, the night garment of a queen. Black ducks are swimming mysteriously on the glowing dusky water.

In a moment, however, the scene has changed and the colours have been withdrawn. The presence in the world, the queen whom we call Day, has passed over the waves and disappeared; not even a fold of the long train of her dress is visible.

Some one has lighted a Roman candle at the far end of the pier, as a signal to a steamer whose white and red lanterns have just been descried upon the dark horizon. It is night: the day is over.

VIII

SUNSET FROM THE GATE OF BAIDARI

IT was at the Gate of Baidari in the Crimea on the shortest day of the year that I saw the most wonderful sunset I have ever known, and entered most completely into the spirit of the dark, quiet night.

It was another vision of the sea, a presentment of the sea's question in a new light.

A mild December afternoon. I had been some days wandering across pleasant tree-brown valleys and immense hollows mountain-walled. In the winter silence there was no murmur of the ocean, not even was there saltness in the air. I was out of the sight of the sea and had been so for several days. But this afternoon I climbed by a long road where were many berberry bushes vermilion with their berries, up to the pass over the hills, and there all at once by surprise, without the least expecting it, at a turn of the road I had a revelation of the whole sea.

It was a ravishment of the eyes, a scene on which one looks, at which one stares. The road came suddenly to a precipice, and sheer down, two thousand feet below, the waves foamed forward on the rocks, and from the foam to the remote horizon lay the mysterious sleeping sea—no, not sleeping, but rather causing all else to sleep in its presence, for it was full of serpent lines all moving toward the shore. The whole wild mountainous Crimean shore sat before the sea and dreamed.

And I realised slowly all that was in the evening. Below me lay the white tortuous road leading downward to the shore in coils, and clothing the road, the many woods, all hoary white because the sharp sea-breeze had breathed on them. Evening had long since settled on the road and on the wintry trees; it lay also about the grey temple which the Russians have put up on one of the platforms of the lower cliffs. The church looked so compact and small down below me that it seemed one could have held it in the palm of the hand. It was sunset, but the sky was full of blue-grey colour. The whole South caught a radiance from the hidden West and the sea was grey.

In a moment it is noticeable that the south is becoming rosier. The sea is now alight from the increase of sunset hues. In the shadow the lines of the sea are a sequence of wavings like the smoke of the snow blown over the steppes. In the hurrying clouds a great space clears, and along the south-west runs a great rosy fleece of sunset. It is rapidly darkening. The sea in the western corner is crimson, but all the vast south is silver and sombre. The horizon is like that seen from a balloon—pushed out to its furthermost, and there, where clouds and sky mingle, one sees fantastically as it were the sides of giant, shadowy fish.

The motor-coach, with its passengers from Sebastopol to Yalta, comes rushing and grumbling up behind me and stops five minutes, this being its half-way point. The passengers adjourn into the inn to drink vodka: "Remember, gentlemen, five minutes only," says the chauffeur. "God help any one who gets left behind at Baidari. . . ." Four minutes later there is a stamping of fat men in heavy overcoats round the brightly varnished 'bus. "Are we going?" says a little man to the refreshed but purple-faced chauffeur. "Yes!" "That's good. I've had enough of this." The guard winds his horn, and after a preliminary squirm of the plump tyres on the soft road, the vehicle and its company goes tumbling down the road as if it were descending into a pit.

And the sunset! It develops with every instant. The lines on the sea seem to move more quickly, and the spaces between them to be larger. The west is full of storm. A closing cloud comes up out of the west: the western sea is utterly hopeless, the moving south inexorable. There is terror in the west.

Evening is more below me than above me. Night is coming to me over the dark woods. The foam on the rocks below is like a milk-white robe. As I walk the first miles downhill I begin to hear the sound of the waves. The sea is beginning to roar, and the wind rushing up to me tells me that the lines of the sea are its stormy waves ridden forward to the shore by a gale.

I stood on the platform where the many-domed temple was built, and watched the gathering night. Unnumbered trees lay beneath me, but it was so dusk I hardly knew them to be trees. The gigantic black cliff that shuts off the west stood blank into the heaven like a great door: to the east lay the ghostly fading coast-line of Aloopka. Among the black clouds overhead danced out happy fires, and, answering their brightness, windows lighted up in cottages far below, and lanterns gleamed on a little steamer just puffing over the horizon.

There came the pure December evening with frost and Christmas bells, and happy hearths somewhere in the background. The one star in the sky was a beckoning one: my heart yearned.

I dipped down upon the road, and in a few minutes was looking at the temple from below, seeing it entirely silhouetted against the sky. It was now indeed held up in a giant's palm and looked at.

Far out at sea now lay a silver strand; the lines of the waves were all curves and heavily laden with shadows—they were, indeed, waves. Far above me the cliffs that I had left were mist-hidden, and in the midst shone a strange light from the last glow of sunset in the unseen west.

Night. At a word the sea became lineless and shapeless. The sunset sky was green-blue, and black strips of cloud lay athwart it. Looking up to the crags above me, I missed the church: it was in heaven or in the clouds. A great wind blew, and ceased, and came no more—the one gust that I felt of a whole day's storm on the coast. Night chose to be calm, and though all the waves called in chorus upon the rocks, there was a silence and a peace within the evening that is beyond all words.

I walked with the night. I walked to find an inn, and yet cared not that the way was far and that men dwelt not in these parts. For something had entered into me from Nature, and I had lived an extra life after the day was done. It was not one person alone that, pack on back, walked that dark and quiet Crimean road. And the new spirit that was with me whispered promises and lingered over secrets half-revealed. I came to know that I should really enter into it, and be one with it, that I should be part of a description of night and part of night itself.

At one of the many turnings of the road I came upon five dreamy waggons, and Tartar waggoners walked by the horses, for their loads were heavy. I made friends with the third waggoner, and he asked me to carry his whip and take his place whilst he talked with one of his mates. For eight miles I walked by the side of the plodding horses, and encouraged them or whipped them, coaxed or scolded them, as they slowly dragged their lumberous merchandise along the dark and heavy roads.

I almost fell asleep, but at an inn half-way I drank tea with the waggoners "cheek by jowl and knee by knee," and they saw me as one of themselves.

Once more on the road—we went nearly all the way to Aloopka. The Tartars sang songs, the beasts of burden toiled; on one side the cliffs overwhelmed us, and on the other lay the dark sea on which the stars were peeping. The still night held us all.

IX

THE MEANING OF THE SEA
I

IT is good to live ever in the sight of the sea. I have been tramping two months along seashores, and living a daily life in the presence of the Infinite. From Nov-orossisk to Batoum, eight hundred and fifty versts, I have explored all that coast of the Black Sea that lies at the feet of the Caucasus—to left of me the snow-peaked mountains shoulder to shoulder under heaven, to right the resplendent, magnificent sea.

"The sea cannot be described," wrote Chekhov; "I once read in a child's copy-book an essay on the sea, four words and a full stop—'The sea is large'—and when-ever I attempt a description, I am obliged to confess that I can do no better than the child." The fact is, the sea describes us; that is why we cannot describe it. It is, itself, language and metaphor for the telling of our own longings and our own mysteries. In the sound of the waves is only the song of man's life; in the endless variety of its appearance only the story of our own mystery.

Thus the sea is all things. They call this the Black Sea, and at evening when the clouds in the high heaven are reflected in it, it is indeed black. But it should be called the many-coloured, for indeed it is all colours. In the full heat of noon, as I write, it is white; it is covered with half-visible vapour through which a greenness is lost in pallor. The horizon is the black line of a broken arc. Other days it is blue as a great ripe plum, and the horizon is faint-pink, like down. On cloudy afternoons it is grey with unmingled sorrow; in early morning it is joyous as a young child. I have seen it from a distance piled up to the sky like a wall of hard sapphire. I have seen it near at hand faint away from the shore, colourless, lifeless, in the heart-searching of its ebb tide. It is all things, at all times, and to all persons.

II

At Dzhugba the sea was quiet as a little lake; at Dagomise it was many-crested and thundering in the majesty of storm. At Gudaout the sun rose over it as it might have done on the first morning of the world.

Every dawning I bathed, and each bathing was as a new baptism. And in multi-farious places it was given to me to bathe; at Dzhugba, where the sun shone fiercely on green water and the dark seaweed washed to and fro on the rocks; at Olginka, the quietest little bay imaginable, where the sea was so clear that one could count the stones below it, the rippling water so crystalline that it tempted one to stoop down and drink—a dainty spot—even the stones, on long curves of the shore, seemed to have been nicely arranged by the sea the night before, and far as I swam out to sea I saw the bottom as through glass.

How different at Dagomise! All night long it had thundered. I slept under a wooden bridge that spanned a dried-up river. The lightning played all about me, the rain roared, the thunder crashed overhead. The storm passed, but as the thunder died away from the sky, it broke out from the sea and roared deafeningly all around. I could not bathe, for the sea was tremendous. A grand sight presented itself at dawn, the sea foaming forwards in thousands of billows. Along five miles of seashore the white horses galloped forward against the rocks, as if the whole sea were an army arrayed against the land. How the white pennons flew!

Later in the morning I undressed, and sitting in moderate safety on a shelf of rock, let the spent billows rush over me. The waves rushed up the steep beach like tigers for their prey, their eyes turned away from mine, but full of cruelty and anger. I was, deep in myself, afear'd.

At what an extraordinary rate the waves rushed up the shore, fast galloping after one another, accomplishing their fates! There is only one line I know that tells well of their rate, that glory of Swinburne:—

Where the dove dipped her wing and the oars won their way, Where the narrowing Symplêgades whiten the straits of Propontis with spray.

III

At Osipovka, where I spent a whole long summer day sitting on a log on the seashore, I saw a vision of the sea and nymphs—a party of peasant girls came down and bathed. They were very pretty and frolicsome, taking to the water in a very different style from educated women. They were boisterous and wild. They went into the sea backwards, and let the great waves knock them down; they lay down and were buffeted by the surf; they ran about the shore, sang, shouted, yelled, waved their arms; they dived headlong into the waves, swam hand over hand among them, pulled one another by the legs. The sea does not know how to play games: it seemed like an ogre with his twelve princesses. They made sport of him, pulled his beard and his hair, tempted and evaded him, mocked him when he grabbed at them, befooled him when he captured them. I used to have an idea of nymphs behaving very artistically with really drawing-room manners, but I saw I was wrong. Nymphs are only artistic and alluring singly—one nymph on a rock before a gallant prince. In numbers they are absolutely wild and have no manners at all. Lucky old ogre, to possess twelve such princesses, I thought; but as I looked at the gleam of their limbs as they mocked, and heard their hard laughter, I found him to be but a pitiable old greybeard, for he looked at beauty that he could scarce comprehend and never possess. The beauty of life has power greater than the beauty of the sea.

IV

One night after I had made my bed on a grassy sand-bank above the sea and was waiting, in the thrilling and breathless twilight, to fall asleep, I suddenly heard a sound as of a child weeping somewhere. My heart bounded in horror. I lay scarce daring to breathe, and then when there was silence again, looked up and down the shore for the person who had cried. But I saw no one. I listened—listened, expecting to hear the cry again, but only the waves turned the stones, broke, rolled up, and turned the stones again. Evening crept over the sea, and the waves looked dark and shadowy; the silence grew more intense. I turned on one side to go to sleep, and then once more came a sad, despairing human cry as of a lost child. I sat bolt upright and looked about me, and even then, whilst I stared, the cry came again, and from the sea. "Is it possible there is a child down by the waves?" I thought, and I tried to distinguish some little human shape in the darkness that seemed hastening on the shoulders of the incoming waves. There came a terrible wail and another silence. I dared not go and search, but I lay and shuddered and felt terribly lonely. The waves followed one another and followed again, ever faster and faster as it seemed in the darkness—

> Still on each wave followed the wave behind,
> And then another behind,
> And then another behind. . . .

They came forward fantastically, and I felt as if I were lying in the presence of something most ancient, most terrible.

Presently a bird with great dark wings flew noiselessly just over my head, and then over the sea rose the moon, young, new drest, and I forgot the strange cry in the presence of a familiar friend. It was as if a light had been brought into one's bedroom. Probably the cry was that of an owl; it came no more. I slept.

V

There was my walk to the forlorn and lonely monastery of Pitsoonda on the promontory where the great lighthouse burns. Along the seashore were swamps overgrown with bamboos and giant grasses, twelve feet high. The sea was grey and calm. Lying on the sand, one saw the reflection, or the refracted images, of the grey stones at the bottom of the sea for twenty yards out and more. The sea had no power, it splashed in weak and hopeless waves, sucked itself away inward, came back again with a little run, and feebly toppled over. The high-water line was shown by a serpentine strip of jetsam winding along the whole of the shore. There was no yellow in the sands; clouds and sunshine struggled overhead, but beneath them all was grey. The wind rustled in the giant grasses like the sound of men on horseback, so that I was continually looking behind in apprehension.

> A land that is lonelier than ruin,
> A sea that is stranger than death.

At a lonely house, half-way to the monastery, I thought to obtain bread, but as I approached it twelve large brown mastiffs rushed out and assailed me. I was in a pitiable plight, warding them off with my stick, and did not escape without bites. I called for help, and some one then whistled from a window and called the dogs back. I don't fear dogs, but these were powerful animals, and withal a tremendous surprise. I must have had a bad time had no one called them away.

I came to the river Bzib, deep and fast-running, and rowed myself across in a leaky and muddy boat. I ploughed my way through deep sand, or stepped from boulder to boulder, or crushed through miles of sea-holly and prickly shrub. I came to the sacred wood in which the Ahkbasians used to pray when they were pagans, but in which, since their conversion, they have chiefly committed murder. I passed through three strange woods, the first of juniper and wild pear; the second, all dead, bleached and impenetrable, of what had once been hawthorn, but now one jagged, fixed mass of awkward arms and cruel thorns; the third, a beautiful, spacious pine-wood, climbing over cliffs to the far verge of the cape where the lighthouse flashes. These were like woods in a fairy tale, and may well have had each their own particular elves and spirits. Each had a separate character: the first as of the earth, homely, full of gentle russet colours from the juniper and the wild fruit; the second, haggish, full of witches whose finger-nails had never been clipped; the third, queenly, as if beloved of Diana.

Evening grew to night as I plodded past these woods or struggled through them. The temptation was to go into the wood and walk on firmer soil—but the thickets were many, and not a furlong did it profit me. Then there were thorns, you must know, and abundant long-clawed creepers that grasped the legs and kept them fixed till they were tenderly extricated by the hand. When I came to the pine-wood it was night, and the many stars shone over the sea. I walked easily and gratefully over the soft pine needles, and I constantly sought with my eyes for the monastery domes. The moonlight through the pines looked like mist, and the forest climbed gradually over rising cliffs. Far away on the dark cape I saw the flash of the lighthouse. . . .

No houses, no people, only a faint cart-track. That track bade me hope. I would follow it in any case. At last, suddenly, I thought I saw the cloud of white smoke of a bonfire. It was the far-away monastery wall, high and white, with a little lamp in one window. I bore up with the distance, forms grew distinct in the night; I entered the monastery by a five-hundred-yard avenue of cedars.

I met a novice in a long smock. He took me to the guest-rooms of the monastery, and there, to my joy, I was accommodated with a bed—the first for many weeks. I was introduced to a very fat and ancient monk who carried at his belt a bunch of keys. Though very stupid, and, as I learnt afterwards, quite illiterate, he was the spirit of hospitality. He kept the larder, and very gladly brought me milk and bread and cheese, roast beef, wine, and would apparently have brought me anything I asked for—all "for the love of God": no monastery charges anything for its hospitality.

After my supper I was glad to stretch my limbs and sleep. I opened my window and lay for a while looking at the mysterious dark masses of the cedars and listening to the low sobbing of the waves. In the monastery buildings I heard the turnings of heavy keys. I slept. Next morning at sunrise I had breakfast in the refectory, and the abbot deigned to come in and talk about Pitsoonda. His was an ancient and beautiful monastery, built by the same hand that erected St. Sophia at Constantinople, Justinian the First. It was indeed a replica of that famous building, a fine specimen of Byzantine architecture. It had changed hands many times, belonging to the Greeks, the Turks, the Cherkesses, and finally to the Russians. Here formerly stood the fortified town of Pitius, scarcely a stone of which was now standing, though many were the weapons and household implements that had been found by the monks. It was now the scene of the quiet life of twenty or thirty brethren. No one ever visited them or sought them from without. Steamers never called—only occasional feluccas came in bringing Caucasian tribesmen from neighbouring villages, and there was no carriage-way to any town.

We talked later of present-day matters, the abbot being at once omniscient and omni-ignorant, and I finished my breakfast in time to accompany him to church. I went to morning service in the great high-walled cathedral and saw all the brothers pray. Of the people of the neighbourhood there were only three; these with the monks formed the whole congregation—there is no village at Pitsoonda. Imagine a gigantic and noble building fit to be the living heart of a great metropolis, and inside of it but a few little pictures, brightly painted, and a diminutive rood-screen, scarcely higher than a five-barred gate. On the ceiling of the great dome was painted a lively and striking picture of Christ, probably done of old time, but in countenance resembling, strangely enough, the accepted portrait of Robert Louis Stevenson—a Christ with a certain amount of cynicism, one who might have smoked upon occasion. No doubt it was painted by a Greek: a Russian would never have done anything so Western.

The monks, looking ancient and dwarf-like, for they had never cut their beards, were accommodated in little pews along the walls, and they could stand and rest their shoulders upon the high arms of the pews and doze, but could not sit, for there were no seats.

The service was beautiful, though I had little feeling of being in church—one needs many people in such a cathedral. I was more interested in the monks, their faces and appearances, and in the atmosphere of the monastery. Most of the monks were peasants, dedicated to the religion of Christ and leading particularly strict lives. It was difficult to understand how they lived. Their faces all bore witness to their religious exercises, and on some were evidences of spiritual meditation. They were all naturally rather stupid, and here more stupid than usual, because they were cut off from society, even from the society of their native villages. They did not study, or read, or write; they had no worldly life to occupy them—there was no means for it. They could gossip—yes, but I doubt if they even did that. Assuredly here the Middle Ages slept.

Round the monastery, behold, the ruins of. a great fort, slowly crumbling away under the hand of Time. No fleets now sail against Pitius, no pirates land on the barren cape—there is nothing to steal. Even the monastery is without gold.

VI

I cannot forget this walk of gloom and mystery, and my stay in this strange, sleeping monastery of the Middle Ages. But over and against it stands the bright morning of Gudaout, four days later.

Gudaout is encompassed by the highest Caucasus—its only refuge is the sea. It is a place most wonderful in the pageantry of dawn. Picture my life of one evening and morning. I left Gudaout at the dusk, and having bought myself a pound of purple grapes, strolled out along the dusty high road eating them. I made my bed on the seashore, and slept away the aches and pains of a heavy day's tramping. Next day, in that sort of reflection of last evening which comes before the morning, I rose, for the coldest of October breezes had come down to me from the mountains. The dawn was all gold—a new dawn, I thought. But when I stood on my feet I saw below the gold the lovely bosom of the East, a beautiful, soft bed of creamy rose. It was an elemental sunrise, a veritable *first* morning.

Distant mountains lay wrapped in dissolving mists, and seemed like the multifarious tents of a great army encamped on a plain—for the smooth sea was like a plain. The chamber of the dawn seemed gigantic, the mountains having lifted up the roof of heaven higher than I had ever seen it before, the sea having taken it out to a far horizon.

I stood looking over the shore before sunrise, and far out in the bay were three high-masted feluccas, looking like ships of the Spanish Armada. At the water's edge, and yet silhouetted against the dawn sky, were Mahometans, washing themselves and praying—stark, black figures in the strange light.

I welcomed the sun.

He rose swiftly out of the waters, and shone across the bay, lighting up all the mountains that closed in north and south. He came full of promises, and after the coolness and damp of the night I had need of heat. I lay on a bank and gleaned sunshine. The morning came over the sea steadily, equably, like a good ship making for a sure harbour.

Then, ten miles from Gudaout, on a mountain, I looked out from the ruins of the Tower of Iver, over a vast resplendent sea, and saw below me the monastery of Novy Afon and all its buildings, looking like children's toys. That tower was a stronghold of Christianity in the third century, and it was strange to think that Crusaders and mediæval warriors had looked out from the same tower, over the same glorious sea. Assuredly from the watch-tower of ancient Time all buildings and man's dwellings are but toys. I thought of that when I rowed across the river Phasis, and drank coffee at Poti on the site of Colchis. That Black Sea and that river were the same which Jason sailed with his heroes; and the Golden Fleece, those children's toy, has now, forsooth, become a head-gear in these parts.

We all pass away, but the sea remains the same; and all our empires and literatures, arts and towns, crumble and decay, and are proved toys. Our consolation lies in our unconquerable souls, our glorious after-life beyond this world. But the sea has an immortality in the here and now. I shall never understand its secret.

A stage is reached when I cease to look at the sea, and allow the sea to look into me, when I give it habitation in my being, and am thereby proved, by virtue of my soul, something mightier than it.

But in vain do we try to take the sea's mystery by storm. In vain do we search for its meaning with love. It lies beyond our mortal ken, deeper than ever plummet sounded.

"Is not the sea the very peacock of peacocks?" asks Nietzsche. "Even before the ugliest of all buffaloes it unfoldeth its tail and never wearieth of its lace fan of silver and gold." But the sea is not moved by slander. "Roll on, thou deep and dark blue ocean, roll!" sings Byron in praise, but the sea is not encouraged. It hearkeneth not, even unto kings. It is that which changes but is itself unchanged. It manifests itself continually in change, and yet it is itself ever the same, ever the same. It reveals itself to man in the majesty and terror of storm, or in the joyousness of peace; when with leaden eye it glowers upward at the leaden clouds, or when the rain sweeps over it in misery. But the secret of the sea lies beyond all these, hidden in the depths, profound, sublime.

II

HOSPITALITY

I

I IMAGINE that whilst the prodigal son sat at meat with his father and their guests, there may have come to the door a weary tramp begging food and lodging. The elder brother would probably refuse hospitality, saying, "You are not even my sinning brother, and shall I harbour *you?*" The father in his wine might cry a welcome—"Let him come in for the sake of my son found this day; he also was a tramp upon the road." The prodigal would say to his steady-going, sober elder, "You say he is not your brother; but he is mine, he is my brother wanderer." "Oh, come in then," the elder brother would retort; "but you must do some work—we can't encourage laziness. You may have shelter and food, but to-morrow you must work with us in the fields till midday."

This counsel of the elder brother has endured, and is accounted wise. But this type of hospitality is not of that sort that was rewarded, say, in Eager Heart. It is scarcely what the writer to the Hebrews intended when he said, "Let brotherly love continue. Be not forgetful to entertain strangers: for thereby some have entertained angels unawares." Of those who wander about the world there are many ordinary men who would be ready to do a morning's work for their board, but there are also gods in disguise. There are mysterious spirits who cannot reveal the necessities of their fate; souls whom if we could recognise in their celestial guise we should worship, falling down at their feet with the humility of the cry, "I am not worthy that thou shouldest come under my roof."

There is another important objection to the complexion of the elder brother's hospitality. Perhaps the tramp would of his own accord have volunteered to work with them next morning. If so, the tramp was deprived of his chance of giving in return. What would have been his gift has been made his price. He should not have been asked to pay. No one asks a brother to pay for food and shelter. And are we not all brothers? True hospitality is a sign of the brotherhood of man, and the open threshold symbolises the open heart. Inhospitality is the sign that man will not recognise the stranger as his brother.

There are two sorts of hospitality, that which gives all it has and that which gives what you want—the former growing out of the latter. The one is prodigal and overflowing generosity, almost embarrassing in its lavishness, the other the simple and ordinary kindness that will always give what it has when there is need; the one the hospitality of Mary who poured out the precious ointment, the other the simple hospitality and homely kindness of Martha; the one is the glory of sacrifice and is of one day in a year or of one day in a life, the other is a sacred due and is of every day. The latter should at least be universal hospitality. It ought to be possible for man to wander where he will over this little world of ours and never fail to find free food and shelter and love. I know no greater shame in national development than the commercialisation of the meal and the night's lodging. It has been our great disinheritance.

But, of course, it would be folly to demand hospitality or to attempt to enforce it. It is like the drunken cobbler who said to his wife, "You don't love me, curse you, but by God you shall if I have to kill you first." Even if a paternal government made a law that hospitality was obligatory and that whoever asked a night's lodging must be given it, then at one blow the whole idea of hospitality would be annihilated. Hospitality must be something freely given, flowing genially outward from the heart. When in the **Merchant of Venice** the Duke says, "Then must the Jew be merciful!" and Shylock asks with true Jewish commercialism, "On what compulsion must I, tell me that?" then Portia gives the eternal answer—

The quality of mercy is not strained,
It droppeth as the gentle rain fom heaven
Upon the place beneath: it is twice blessed;
It blesseth him that gives and him that takes.

Need it be said mercy and hospitality are in many respects one and the same, and that when Portia says, "We do pray for mercy and that same prayer doth teach us all to render the deeds of mercy," it is like saying, "We pray for hospitality in heaven and that prayer teaches us to render hospitality here," like "Forgive us our trespasses as we forgive them that trespass against us." We shall never be homeless, either here or hereafter, if we love one another.

The shelter and food given one for the love of God are "sanctified creatures." Sleeping in a home for the love of God is more refreshing than sleeping at an inn for a price. One has been blessed and one has also blessed in return; for again, hospitality, like mercy, blesses both those who give and those who take. Throughout a night one has helped to constitute a home, and the angels of the home have guarded one. One has lain not merely in a house but in a Christian home, not only in a home but in the temple of the heart.

It is sweet in a far-away land to be treated like a son or a brother, to be taken for granted, to be embraced by strange men and blessed by strange women. Sweet also is it for the far-away man to recognise a new son or a new brother in the wanderer whom he has received. I remember one night at the remote village of Seraphimo in Archangel Government, how a peasant put both hands on my shoulders and, looking into my eyes, exclaimed, "How like he is to us!"

II

Tramping across the Crimean moors I lost my way in the mist near the monastery of St. George, and was conducted by a peasant to the Greek village of Kalon, well known to old campaigners—it is between Sebastopol and Balaklava. The village remains the same today as it was in the days of the Crimean War, and the same families as lived there then, or their descendants, live there now. I visited the **sta-rosta,** and he indicated a home where I might sleep the night. I was taken in by an aged Greek woman and entertained among her family. They brought me bread and wine, and spread out the best couch for me. The sons told me of hunting exploits with the bear and the wild boar; they told me how at Christmas time the wild turkeys fly overhead in such numbers that it is the easiest thing in the world to shoot one's Christmas dinner—and I thought that very convenient. When the sons were silent, or talking among themselves, the old dame told me about her youth: how she was only seventeen years old at the time of the war; how the English were the most handsome of all the soldiers, how the Turks were the most lazy and the most brutal, how the French and the Italians simpered; how the English soldiers were loved by the Greek girls, how they were also more generous than the other troops and gave freely clothes and tea and sugar and whatever was needed in the cottages and asked no money for it whatever; how in these days the little children played with the cannon-balls, rolling them over the moors and up the village street—all manner of gossip the good old lady told me, beguiling the hours and my ears till it was bedtime. Next day I offered to pay at least for my food, but the old lady, though poor, waved her hand and said, "Oh no, it is for the love of God!" How often have I had that said to me day after day in Russia, especially in the North!

Another day in Imeritia, when I passed at evening through a little Caucasian village and was beginning to wonder where I should have my supper and find a night's lodging, a Georgian suddenly hailed me unexpectedly. He was sitting, not in his own house, but at a table in an inn. There were of course no windows to the inn, and all the company assembled could easily converse with the horsemen and pedestrians in the street below. He called out to me and I went up to him. A place was made for me at the table, and he ordered a chicken and a bottle of wine. I was just a little doubtful, for I had never seen the man before and his anticipation of my needs was surprising, but I accepted his invitation, drank his health, and ate my meal. He looked at me very pleasantly, and he was more sensible than a Russian, the sort of person who is marvellously interested in you, but who is so gentle that he will ask no questions lest you find some pain in answering him. But I told him about myself. After the meal he took me along to his house and gave me a spare bed. All was very disorderly and he apologised, saying, "It is untidy, but I am a bachelor. What is a bachelor to do? If I were married all would be different." I spent a whole day with him, and in that short space he conceived for me as it seemed an eternal friendship.

"You are very good," I said at parting. "You have been very hospitable. I don't know how to thank you. . . ." He stopped my words. "No, no," he said, "it is only natural; it is no doubt what any one would do for me in your country were I a stranger there."

"Would they?" I thought.

By the way, a curious example of inhospitality showed itself in this village where I met the Georgian. We were sitting round a pitcher of sweet rose-coloured wine, and one of us signalled to a rather morose Akhbasian prince who was passing, but he took no notice. "He will not drink wine with us," said my friend. "His wife is so beautiful."

"What do you mean?" I asked.

"His wife is very beautiful and he is as jealous of her as she is beautiful. He is like a dog who growls when he has suddenly got something very good in his mouth: he fears any familiarity on the part of other dogs."

As a tramp I have often felt how little I had to give materially for all the kindness I have received. But even such as myself have their opportunities of reciprocity, though they are of a humble kind. I call to mind a cold, wet day near Batoum, how I had a big bonfire by a' stream under a bridge and I warmed myself, cooked food, and took shelter from the rain. A Caucasian man and woman, both tramps, came and sat by my fire a long while. The man took from his breast some green tobacco leaves, dried them by the fire, and put them in his pipe and smoked them.

They spoke a language quite unintelligible to me and knew not a word of Russian. But they were nevertheless extremely demonstrative and told me all manner of things by signs and gestures. Very poor, even starving, and I gave them some bread and beef and some hot rice pudding from my pot. In return the man gave me five and a half walnuts! We seemed like children playing at being tramps, but I felt a very lively affection for these strange wanderers who had come so trustingly to my little home under the bridge.

One of the beautiful things about hospitality is that though we do not pay the giver of it directly, we do really pay him in the long run. A is hospitable to B, B to C, C to D, and so on, and at last Z is hospitable to A. It is largely a matter of "Forgive us our trespasses as we forgive them that trespass against us." It is significant that the Russian's parting word equivalent to our "God be with you "is "Forgive!"

III

When St. Peter said to the beggar, "Silver and gold have I none, but such as I have give I thee," it is not to be thought that he hadn't a few coppers to spare. He meant, "Silver and gold are not my gifts; I have something other and more precious." Thus the apostle indicated the deeper significance of charity.

There is hospitality of the mind as well as of the hand, though both spring from the heart. Hospitality of the hand is having a home with open doors, but that of the mind is having open the temple of the soul.

I once called upon a hermit and we talked of the significance of hospitality. At last he said to me: "You praise hospitality well, my brother, but there is another and a greater hospitality than you have yet mentioned. It is the will to take the wanderer not only into the house to feed but into the heart to comfort and love, the ability to listen when others are singing, to see when others are showing, to understand when others are suffering. It is what the writer to the Corinthians meant by charity.

"Thus—'Though I speak with the tongues of men and of angels, and have not charity, I am become as sounding brass, or a tinkling cymbal,' is like saying, 'Though I have all possible eloquence and yet do not understand mankind, do not take him to my heart, I am as sounding brass; unless my eloquence is music played upon the common chord I am but a tinkling cymbal.'

" 'And though I have the gift of prophecy, and understand all mysteries, and all knowledge; and though I have all faith, so that I could remove mountains, and have not charity, I am nothing,' is like saying, 'Though I see into the future but misunderstand its significance; though I understand all mysteries, but not the mystery of the human heart; though I am able to remove obstacles by faith, I am simply like Napoleon, finishing up at St. Helena, I am nothing.'

" 'And though I bestow all my goods to feed the poor, and though I give my body to be burned, and have not charity, it profiteth me nothing,' is like saying, 'Organised philanthropy is not charity, neither is the will to be a martyr, unless these things spring from the will to feel how our brothers suffer.'

" 'Charity suffereth long, and is kind; charity envieth not; charity vaunteth not itself, is not puffed up, doth not behave itself unseemly, seeketh not her own, is not easily provoked, thinketh no evil;

" 'Rejoiceth not in iniquity, but rejoiceth in the truth,' for the truth refutes all uncharitable judgment, the truth shows us all as brothers, shows us all needing the love which one man can give to another.

" 'Charity beareth all things, believeth all things, hopeth all things, endureth all things. Charity never faileth' "

I understood the hermit though it seemed to me there was much that he left out. Had he been a tramp instead of a hermit he would probably have thought as I do. The world that he talked of was obviously one entirely of men and women, and he left out of account all that world which we call Nature.

It is well to receive men and shelter them and feed them, and well to understand their hearts, but when men are not near there is another beautiful world knocking at our doors and asking hospitality in our souls; it is the world of Nature. Oh ye young of all ages, be hospitable unto Nature, open your doors to her, take her to your hearts! She will rebuild your soul into a statelier mansion, making for herself a fitting habitation, she will make you all beautiful within. Then, when you extend the hospitality of your hearts, your ***temples,*** to man, they will be spacious temples and rich hearts. Nature comes first, for she heals hearts' wounds; if you have not received her communion first you will not be so fit to receive man. The consumptive-bodied already go to the country, and we are nearly all of us, in this era of towns, consumptive-souled. We need whole hearts just as we need whole lungs. But what am I saying? I am bidding you bargain with Nature for a price, and that is wrong. You must love her, not for anything she can give you. What is more, you can never know what she will give you: she may even take away. When you see her you will love her as a bride. Be receptive to her beauty, be always Eager Heart. When any man receives her into himself there is born in his soul's house the baby Christ, the most wonderful and transfiguring spirit that man has yet known upon a strange world.

II

THE STORY OF THE RICH MAN AND THE POOR MAN

ON my way to Jerusalem I tramped through a rich residential region where wealthy Armenians, Turks, and Russians dwelt luxuriously in beautiful villas looking over the sea. I had been sleeping out, for the road was high and dry and healthy, but at last, entering a malarial region, I began to seek shelter more from man than from Nature.

One cold and cloudy night I came into the village of Ugba and sought hospitality. There were few houses and fewer lights, and some feeling of awkwardness, or perhaps simply a stray fancy, prompted me to do an unusual thing—to beg hospitality at one of the luxurious villas. I had nearly always gone to the poor man's cottage rather than to the rich man's mansion, but this night, the opportunity offering, I appealed to the rich.

I came to the house of a rich man, and as I saw him standing in the light of a front window I called out to him from a distance. In the dusk he could not make out who I was, but judging by my voice he took me for an educated man, one of his own class.

"Can you put me up for the night?" I asked.

"Yes," he replied cheerfully. "Come round by the side of the house, otherwise the dogs may get in your way."

But when the rich man saw me on his threshold a cloud passed over his eyes and the welcome faded from his face. For I was dressed simply as a tramp and had feet so tired that I had not troubled to take the signs of travel from my garments. I had a great sack on my back, and in my hand a long staff.

The head of the house, a portly old gentleman with a long beard, interrogated me; his son, a limp smiling officer in white duck, peered over his shoulder; two or three others of the establishment looked on from various distances.

"What do you want?" asked the old gentleman curtly, as if he had not heard, already.

"A lodging for the night," I said unhappily.

"You won't find lodging here," said the greybeard in a false stentorian voice. And the little officer in white giggled.

"You've made a mistake and come to the wrong house. We have no room."

"A barn or outhouse would serve me nicely," I put in.

The old man waved his hand.

"No, no. You are going southward? You have strayed somewhat out of your path coming up here. There is a short cut to the main road. There you'll find a tavern."

It was in my mind to say, "I am an Englishman, a traveller and writer, and I am on a pilgrimage to Jerusalem. You misdoubt my appearance, and are afraid of sheltering an unknown wanderer, but I am one whom you would find it interesting and perhaps even profitable to harbour." But my heart and lips were chilled.

I had taken off my pack, but put it on again humbly and, somewhat abashed, prepared to leave. The family stood by staring. It was a very unusual thing for a poor tramp to come and ask hospitality. Tramps as a rule knew better than to come to their doors. Indeed, no tramp had ever come there before. It rather touched them that I should have believed they would shelter me. Their refusal troubled them somewhat.

"There's always plenty of room in the tavern," said the rich man to his wife. "And they'll be glad to have a customer."

As I turned to go, some one brought a light, and a gleam fell on my face. The company expected to see the cringing, long-suffering face of a peasant in the presence of his master, but the light showed something different. . . .

"He is perhaps one of our own class . . . or . . . God knows what . . ." they thought, one and all. "It is hateful to have refused him. But no, if he is one of us, why does he come clothed like a common man? He has only himself to blame."

The old man, feeling somewhat ashamed, offered to show me the way. He came out and pointed out the short cut to the tavern.

"It is quite clear. I shall find the way," I said. "Thank you."

The old man halted as if he wished to say something more.

"What now?" I asked myself. I said good-bye, and as I moved away he asked:

"You are going far, belike!"

"To Jerusalem," I answered laconically. In Russia there is only one thing to say when a man tells you he is going to Jerusalem. It is, "Pray for me there!" But somehow that request stuck in the old man's throat.

When I got outside the park gates I pulled down my pack and took out of it the only thing that had stood between me and a night's lodging—a grey tweed sportsman's jacket—and I put it on, and with it a collar and tie, and I walked along the road in real sadness. For I felt wounded.

I could forgive the man for doing so unto me, but it was hard to forgive him for doing so unto himself, unto us all. He had made life ugly for a moment, and made the world less beautiful. To-morrow the sun and the earth would be less glorious because of him.

But I had only walked a few steps down the road from the rich man's house when I came to a poor peasant's hut where there burned one little light at a little square window.

And I thought, "Please God, I will not go to the tavern, which is possibly kept by a Turk and is very dirty. I will try for a night's lodging here."

I knocked at the door with my staff.

There was a stirring inside.

"Who is there?"

"One who wants a lodging for the night. It is late to disturb you, but I fear there will be rain."

A peasant woman came to the door and unbarred it, and let me in.

"Ah, little father," she said, "you come late, and we have little space, as you see, only one room and a big family, but come in if you will."

She turned up the little kerosene lamp and looked at me.

"Ai, ai," she said, "a ***barin.***" She looked at my coat and collar. "It will be but poor fare here."

"Not a ***barin,***" I urged, "but a poor wanderer coming from far and going farther still. I generally sleep under the open sky with God as my host and the world as my home, but to-night promises storm, and I fear to take cold in the rain."

The peasant girl, for she was no more, busied herself with the samovar. "You must have something hot to drink, and some milk and eggs perhaps. My husband is not yet home from market, but he will come belike very soon, and will be very glad to find a stranger. He will rejoice. He always rejoices to give hospitality to strangers upon the road."

When she had brought me a' meal she fetched fresh hay from a barn and spread a quilt over it and made a bed for me, and would have given me her own pillow but that I pointed out that my pack itself made a very good resting-place for my head.

Then her husband came home, a strong kindly man, full of life and happiness, and he did rejoice as his little wife had promised. He was sorry he had not wine with which to entertain me. Such people drink wine not more than twice in a year.

And with these humble, gentle folk I forgot the rich man's coldness, and healed my heart's wounds. Life was made beautiful again. Tomorrow the sun would be as bright as ever.

I slept in the comfortable warm bed on the floor of the poor peasant's hut, and the storm rolled overhead, the winds moaned and the rain fell.

"You are going to Jerusalem," said the good man and woman next morning, "pray for us there. It is hard for us to leave our little hut and farm, or we would go to the Holy Land ourselves. We should like to go to the place where the Christ was born in Bethlehem and to the place where He died."

"I shall pray," I said; and I thought in my heart, "They are there in Jerusalem all the time, even though they remain here. For they show hospitality to strangers."

But as I trudged along my way there seemed to be a pathos too deep for tears underlying my experiences at the hands of the rich man and of the poor man.

That it should occur so in real life, and not merely in a moral tale!

The position of the rich man is so defensible. Of course it would have been ridiculous of him to have sheltered me. Who was I? I had no introduction. What was I? I might have robbed him in the night . . . or murdered. I was ill-dressed and poor, therefore no doubt covetous of his fine clothes and wealth. They would only have themselves to blame if they sheltered me and I did them harm. Besides, was there not the tavern close by? All reason pointed to the tavern.

But something troubled them, something in my face and demeanour!

Alas for such people! They forget that Christ comes into this world not clothed in purple. They forget that Christ is always walking on the road, and that he shows himself as one needing help. And always once in a man's life the pilgrim Christ comes knocking at his door, with the pack of man's sorrows on his back and in his hand the staff which may be a cross.

I met the young officer in white next morning. He looked at me with a certain amount of surprise. I hailed him.

"Did you sleep well at the tavern?" he asked.

"I found shelter at a peasant's house," I answered.

"Ah! That's well. I didn't think of that. You said you were going to Jerusalem. Why is that? Evidently you are not Russian."

I told him somewhat of my plans. He seemed interested and somewhat vexed. "I said we ought to have taken you in," he said apologetically. "But you came so late—'like a thief in the night,' as the Scripture saith."

I sat down on a stone and laughed and laughed. He stared at me in perplexity.

" 'Like a thief in the night,' " I cried out. "Oh, how came you to hit on that expression? Go on, please—'and I knew you not.' Who is it who cometh as a thief in the night?"

The officer smiled faintly. He was dull of understanding, but evidently I had made a joke, or perhaps I was a little crazed.

He turned on his heel. "Sorry we turned you away," he repeated, "but there are so many scoundrels about. If you're passing our way again be sure and call in. Come whilst it's light, however."

III

A LODGING FOR THE NIGHT

DZHUGBA is an aggregation of cottages and villas round about the estuary of a little river flowing down from the Caucasus to the Black Sea. On the north a long cliff road leads to Novorossisk a hundred miles, and southward the same road goes on to Tuapse, some fifty miles from Maikop and the English oil-fields.

I arrived at the little town too late to be sure of finding lodging. The coffee-house was a wild den of Turks, and I would not enter it; most private people were in bed. I walked along the dark main street and wondered in what unusual and unexpected manner I should spend the night. When one has no purpose, there is always some real *providence* waiting for the tramp.

The quest of a night's lodging is nearly always the origin of mysterious meetings. It nearly always means the meeting of utter strangers, and the recognition of the fact that, no matter how exteriorly men are unlike one another, they are all truly brothers, and have hearts that beat in unison. Thus did it happen that I met my strange host of Dzhugba.

A hatless but very hairy Russian met me at a turning of the road, and eyeing me with lack-lustre eyes asked me gruffly as a rude shopman might, "What do you want?"

"A lodging for the night."

The peasant reflected, as if mentally considering the resources of the little town. At last after a puzzling silence he put one fat hand on my shoulder, and staring into my face, pronounced his verdict—

"The houses are all shut up and the people gone to bed. There is no place; even the coffee-house is full. But never mind, you can spend the night in a shed over here. I shall find you a place. No, don't thank me; it comes from the heart, from the soul."

He led me along to a lumber-room by the side of the plank pier. It contained two dozen barrels of "Portlandsky" cement. The floor was all grey-white and I looked around some-what dubiously, seeing that cement is rather dirty stuff to sleep upon. But, nothing a-bashed, my new friend waved his hand as if showing me into a regal apartment.

"Be at your ease!" said he. "Take whatever place you like, make yourself comfortable, No, no thanks; it is all from God, it is what God gives to the stranger."

He thereupon ran out on to the sand, for the shed was on the seashore, and he beckoned me to follow. To my astonishment, we found out there an old rickety bedstead with a much rent and rusted spring mattress—apparently left for me providentially. It was so old and useless that it could not be considered property, even in Russia. It belonged to no one. Its nights were over. I gave it one night more.

The peasant was in high glee.

"Look what I've found for you," said he. "Who could have expected that to be waiting outside for you? Several days I have looked at that bedstead and thought, 'What the devil is that skeleton? Whence? Whither?' Now I understand it well. It is a bed, the bed of the Englishman on the long journey. . . ."

The mattress was fixed to an ancient bed frame—one could not call it bedstead—with twisted legs that gave under weight and threatened to break down. We brought the "contrapshun" in.

"Splendid!" said my host.

"Impossible," I thought, trying to press down the prickly wire where the mattress was torn.

"No doubt you are hungry," my friend resumed. I assured him I was not in the least hungry, but despite my protestations he ran off to bring me something to eat. I felt sorry; for I thought he might be bringing me a substantial supper, and I had already made a good meal about an hour before. What was more, he lived at some distance, and I did not care to trouble the good man, or for him to waken up his wife who by that hour was probably sleeping.

However, he was gone, and there was nothing to be done. I laid some hay on the creaking sorrow of a bed, and endeavoured to bend to safety the wilderness of torn and rusty wire. I spread my blanket over the whole and gingerly committed my body to the comfortable-seeming couch. Imagine how the bed became an unsteady hammock of wire and how the contrivance creaked at each vibration of my body. I lay peacefully, however, looked at the array of cement barrels confronting me, and waited for my host. I expected a plate of chicken and a bottle of wine, and was gradually feeling myself converted to the idea that I wouldn't mind a nice tasty supper even though I had made my evening meal.

What was my astonishment when the good man returned bearing a square-foot slice of black bread on which reposed a single yellow carrot! I looked curiously at the carrot, but my host said, *"Nitchevo, nitchevo, vinograd"*—"Don't worry, don't worry, a grape, that's all."

He had also brought a kerosene lamp, which, however, lacked a glass. He stood it on one of the grey barrels and turned it monstrously high, just to show his largeness of heart, I suppose. I got up and turned it down because it was smoking, and he waved his hand once more deprecatingly, and turning the wick up and down several times, signified that I was to do with it exactly as I pleased, He left it smoking again, however.

I put the thought of a good supper out of my mind and looked at the black bread with some pathos, as who would not after conjuring before the eyes a plate of chicken and a bottle of wine? However, it was indeed **nitchevo,** to use the Russian phrase, a mere nothing. I averred I was not hungry and put the bread in my pack, of which I had made a pillow, and simulating comfort, said I thanked him and would now go to sleep. My host understood me, but was not less original in his parting greeting than in the rest. He shook hands with me effusively, and pointed to the roof.

"One God," he said. "And two men underneath. Two men, one soul."

He looked at me benevolently and pointed to his heart.

"Two men, one soul," he repeated, and crossed himself. "You understand?"

"I understand."

Then he added finally, "Turn the lamp as high as you like," and suited the action to the word by turning it so high that one saw a dense cloud of smoke beyond the lurid flame.

"Good-night!"

"Good-night!"

My queer guardian angel disappeared. I fastened the door so that it should not swing: in the wind, and then climbed back into my wire hammock, stretched out my limbs, laid my cheek on my pack, and slept.

Nothing disturbed me, though I woke in the night, and looking round, missed the Ikon lamp which would have been burning had I been in a home. It was a saint's day. The absence of the Ikon told me the difference between sleeping in a house and sleeping in a home. Perhaps it was because of this difference that my host blessed me so earnestly.

Next morning I sought my host in vain. He had apparently left the town before dawn with a waggon of produce that had to be carted to Tuapse. At breakfast in the Turkish coffeehouse I looked with some amusement at the bread and carrot, discarded the latter, but munched the former to the accompaniment of a plate of chicken and a bottle of wine. My imagining, therefore, of the previous night was not altogether vain. All that was needed was that my comical host should look in. As it was, in his absence I drank his health with a Georgian.

IV

SOCRATES OF ZUGDIDA

I WAS travelling without a map, never knowing what I was coming to next, what long Caucasian settlement or rushing unbridged river, and I came quite unexpectedly to a town. I had not the remotest idea that a town was near, and when I learned the name of the town I realised that I had never heard of it before—Zugdida.

This is no fairy story. Zugdida veritably exists, and may be found marked on large maps. I came into it on a Sunday evening, and found it one of the largest and most lively of all the Caucasian towns I had yet visited; the shops and the taverns all open, the wide streets crowded with gaily dressed horsemen, the footways thronged with peasants walking out in Sunday best. A remote town withal, not on the railways, and unvisited as yet by any motor-car—unvisited, because the rivers in these parts are all bridgeless.

I was looking for a place where I might spend the night—towns are inhospitable places, and one is timorous of sleeping in a tavern full of armed drunkards—when I was hailed by a queer old man, who noticed that I was a stranger. He kept one of the two hundred wine-cellars of the town, and was able to give me a good supper and a glass of wine with it. He was an aged Mingrelian, bald on his crown, but lank-haired, dreamy-eyed, stooping; he had a Robinson Crusoe type of countenance. I had come to one of the oldest inhabitants of Zugdida, an extraordinary character.

I asked him how the town had grown in his memory.

"When I came here from the hills forty years ago," said he, "long before the Russo-Turkish War, there were three houses here—three only, two were wine-cellars. Now Zugdida is second only to Kutais. I remember how two more wine-cellars were built, and a small general shop, then a bread shop, then two more wine-cellars, two little grocer's shops, some farm-houses. We became a fair-sized village, and wondered how we had grown. The Russians came and built stone houses and a military barracks, a prison, a police-station, and a big church; then came the Hotel of Russia, the Universal Stores. We built the broad, flag-stoned market, and named a Fair day; saddlery and sword shops opened, blacksmiths, gunsmiths, coppersmiths, jewel workers, tailors; Singer's sewing machines came, two more hotels, and we grew and grew. We have now over two hundred taverns. We have offered the Government to pay for all the necessary land, and defray all minor expenses, if they will connect us with Poti by railway, and if it were not that so many people want bribes we should be part of Europe. As it is, we're just a bit of the old Caucasus."

He pointed to a group of drunkards, all armed from head to foot, but now clinging to one another and raising their voices in Asiatic chanting.

After supper—a stew of mutton and maize, with a bottle of very sweet rose-coloured wine—the old man took me aside and made me a long harangue on life and death and the hereafter. Better sermon on a Sunday evening I never heard in church. He told me the whole course of the good man's life and compared it with that of the bad man, weighed the two, and found the latter wanting on all counts, adding, however, that it was impossible to be good.

"How did you come to think so seriously of life?" I inquired.

"In this way," he replied. "Once I was very 'flee-by-the-sky'—I didn't care a rap, sinned much, and feared neither God nor the devil—or, if anything, I feared the devil a little; for God I never had the least respect. But one day I picked up a book written by one Andrew, and I read some facts that astonished me. He said that in eight thousand years after the creation of the world the sun would go red and the moon grey, the sun would grow old and cease to warm the world—just as you and I must inevitably grow old. In that day would be born together, one in the East and one in the West, Christ and the Anti-Christ, and they would fight for the dominion of the world. This story caused me to pause and think. Hitherto I had taken all for granted. It had never occurred to me that the sun might stop shining, that the stars might go out. I had scarcely thought that I myself might stop, might die.

" 'What happens to me when I die?' I asked people. 'God will judge you,' they said. 'If good, you go to heaven; if evil, to hell.' That did not satisfy me. How did people know? No one had ever come back to tell us how things were done after death.

"I had never thought at all before, but now I began to think so hard that I could not go about the ordinary things of life, I was so wrapped up in the mystery of my own ignorance.

"People said I was under the evil eye. But that again was nonsense. 'Whence comes man?' I asked. 'Where does he go? Where was I before I was born?' I was part of my ancestors. Very well. 'But where shall I go when I die? What shall I be?'

"I nearly learned to disbelieve in religion. You must know I began to go to church every Saturday evening and on all festivals. I listened intently to all the services and the sermons, and I read all that I could find to read, and I asked questions of priests and of educated people—all with the idea of solving this mystery of life. I tried to be good at the bidding of the Church, but I gave that up. I learned that it was impossible to avoid sin.

"You drink wine—this is a sin; give short weight—that is a sin; look on your neighbour's wife—that is a sin; everything you do is sin—even if you do nothing, that is sin; there is no road of sinlessness.

"I went on living as I felt inclined, without care as to whether it were sin or no. But still I asked myself about man's life.

"Some one said to me, 'You will never understand, because you think of your-self as a separate individual, and not as just a little part of the human race. You live on in all the people who come after you, just as before you were born you lived in those who were before you.'

"That was something new, but I understood him, and I asked him a new ques-tion: 'If what you say is true—and very likely it is—what, then, is the past of the whole human race, and what its future? What does the life of the human race mean?'

"That he could not answer. Can you answer it? No. No one can answer it."

"You are like Socrates," I said.

"Who was Socrates?"

"He was the man whom the Oracle indicated as the wisest man alive. All men knew nothing, but Socrates was found wiser than they, for he alone knew that he knew nought."

A look of pleased vanity floated over the face of my Mingrelian host. He was at least quite human.

Before going to bed we drank one another's healths.

V

"HAVE YOU A LIGHT HAND?"

THIS is not simply a matter of making pastry, as you shall see.

I was tramping along a Black Sea road one night, and was wondering where I should find a shelter, when suddenly a little voice cried out to me from the darkness of the steppe. I stopped and looked and listened. In a minute a little boy in a red shirt and a grey sheepskin hat came careering towards me, and called out: "Do you want a place to sleep? My mother's coffee-house is the best you'll find. The coffeehouse down the hill is nothing to it. There it is, that dark house you passed. I am out gathering wood for the fire, but I shall come in a minute."

Sharp boy! He was only eight years old. How did he guess my need so well?

I retraced my footsteps very happily, and came to the dark inn I had missed. It stood fifty yards back from the road, and had no light except what glimmered from the embers of a wood fire. At the door was a parrot that cried out, "Choozhoï, choozhoï, choozhoï preeshòl"—"A stranger, a stranger, a stranger has arrived."

The mother, a pugnacious gossip with arms akimbo, looked at me with perturbed pleasure. "Are you a beggar or a customer?" she asked. "Because if you're a beggar," etc. I cut her short as soon as I could. I assured her I should be much pleased to be a customer.

I ordered tea. The boy came in and claimed me as his find, but was snubbed. My hostess proceeded to ask me every question known to her. To my replies, which were often not a little surprising, she invariably replied with one of these exclamations, "Say it again, if you please." "Indeed!" "With what pleasure!"

That I was a tramp and earned my living by writing about my adventures pleased her immensely. I earned my living by having holidays, and gained money where other travellers never did anything but spend. "With what pleasure" did she hear that literary men were paid so many roubles a thousand words for their writings. One could easily write an immense quantity, she thought.

The little boy looked at me with bright eyes, and listened. Presently, when his mother was dilating on the inferiority of painting as a profession, he broke in.

The mother was saying, "Not only does the painter catch cold standing still so long in marshy places, but when he has finished his pictures he has to hawk them in the fairs, and even then he may not be able to sell them."

"What fairs?" asked the boy.

"The fairs of Moscow, Petersburg, Kiev, and the great towns. Some sell for fifty roubles, some for five hundred, some for five thousand and more. A little picture would go for five roubles perhaps."

"What size pictures would one buy for fifty roubles?" asked the boy.

"Oh, about the same size as from the floor to the ceiling."

"What size would one be that cost five thousand roubles?"

"Oh, an immense picture; one could build a country house out of it."

The boy reflected.

"And five hundred thousand roubles?" he asked. But his mother remained profitably silent over the preparation of the family soup. The fire now blazed with the additional wood that had been heaped upon it. The little voice repeated the absurd question, and the mother shouted, "Silence! Don't make yourself a nuisance."

"But how big would it be?" whined the boy. "Tell me."

"Oh, the same, but bigger, stupid!"

Thereupon my little friend was very happy, and he apparently ascribed his happiness to me.

A few minutes later he abruptly asked permission to take me up a mountain to show me a castle next morning, and his mother agreed, pointing out how extremely profitable it would be for me. The little boy rejoiced; he had apparently wanted to go up to that castle for a long while. How excited and happy he was!

His mother paid little attention to her child, however, and her interest lay in the bubbling cauldron where the soup was cooking. "You have a very clever boy," I said, but she did not agree with me. His pranks and high spirits were to her evidence of stupidity. I must say I felt we were the stupid party, and the boy was a little wonder. We went on gossiping, and presently he proved us stupid.

He started up with one finger to his ear and then darted out, leaving the door open and letting the steppe air pour in.

The mother listened, and then said discontentedly after a pause, "That child is not usual."

The boy came back with fifteen shaggy customers, however; fifteen red-faced waggoners, half-frozen in their sheepskins, and all clamoured for food and drink.

The boy, all excitement, danced up to me and said, "Have you a light hand? You must have a light hand!" I didn't know what he meant, but he was off before I had time to ask.

He began serving tea and cutting bread and asking questions. Did any one want soup? Nobody wanted soup at first, but at the boy's solicitations nine of them agreed to have portions at twopence a plateful. The mother persuaded others to have pickled herrings,

cheese, wine.

The inn was of two rooms: one a bedroom and retiring-room without a door The Ikon of this room served the economical hostess for both rooms.

The waggoners were all surly till they had fed. "Show me where we can bow to God," said one of them very gruffly, not seeing the Ikon. The little boy led him and all his mates into the little bedroom, and they all bowed their hairy faces and crossed themselves before the Ikon of St. Nicholas.

Then they returned and consumed the soup and the herrings and bread and cheese and wine and tea. I looked on. My hostess was turning a pretty penny. I was looking on at a very pleasant and surprising interlude.

Every now and then one of the mouzhiks would stump out to see how the horses were, for they had a long train of waggons carrying building materials to the Tsar's estate of Livadia. At length all had supped, and they came up to the counter one by one and thanked the hostess heartily, paying her the while.

Only one of the men was dissatisfied—the last one to come up.

"Your soup is dear," said he.

"Dear! What do you mean?" said the woman. "How much would you pay for such soup in Yalta, and with beef at fivepence a pound, too?"

"In Yalta they give one soup."

"And here!"

"Here . . . as God wills . . . something . . . ." The mouzhik slammed the door.

"There's a man," said my hostess, but she wasn't enraged. Had she not just sold the family's soup for eighteenpence, and made ten-pence profit on it, and wouldn't her husband be pleasantly surprised when he saw there were three shillings more on the counter than usual? It was not often that such custom had come to her.

The boy explained the reason to her in a whisper: "He has a light hand."

"Very like," said she, looking at me with new interest.

"What do you mean?" I asked the boy.

"Why, don't you know?" said he wonderingly. "Wherever you go you bring good fortune. After I met you on the road I immediately began to find wood much more plentifully. When I came in I learned how to buy pictures. Then mother said she would let me go with you to see the castle. Then, not only are you a good customer staying the night, but after you came all this crowd of customers. Generally we have nobody at all. . . ."

"And I met this wonderful boy," thought I. "I should like to carry him away. He is like something in myself. He also had the light hand, but what a testimony he gave the tramp! Wherever he goes he brings happiness."

As once I wrote before, "tramps often bring blessings to men: they have given up the causes of quarrels. Sometimes they are a little divine. God's grace comes down upon them."

VI

ST. SPIRIDON OF TREMIFOND

THE charge for driving on Caucasian roads is a penny per horse per mile, so if you ride ten miles and have two horses you pay the driver one shilling and eightpence. But if, as generally happens, the driver's sense of cash has deprived him of a sense of humour, a conversation of this kind commonly arises.

"One and eightpence. What's this?

"Ten miles, and two horses at a penny per horse per mile; isn't that correct?"

"To the devil with your one and eightpence. Give it to the horses; a penny a mile for a horse, and how about the man, the cart, the harness? I gave you hay to sit on. See what fine weather it has been! What beautiful scenery! Yonder is the church . . . the wineshop, the . . ."

"Hold hard, my good man. The Universe, our salvation by Christ, why don't you charge for these as well! Here's sixpence to buy yourself a drink."

The driver takes the sixpence and looks at it, makes a calculation, and then blurts out:

"What! Sixpence for a man and tenpence for a horse; ai, ai, what a **barin** I have found. Sixpence for a man and tenpence for a horse. Bad news, bad news! Cursed be the day. . . ."

Here you give him another sixpence, and get out of earshot quickly.

A penny a mile a horse. It is good pay in the Caucasus, and I for my part charge myself only a halfpenny a mile. If I walk twenty-five miles, then I allow myself a shilling wages, and, of course, some of that I save for the occasion when I come into a town with a great desire for good things. Then a spending of savings and a feast!

"Good machines use little fuel," said an emaciated tramp to me one day. But I have no ambition to be accounted a good machine on those terms. I eat and drink anything that comes in my way, and am ready at any moment to feast or to fast. I seldom pass a crab-apple tree without tasting its fruit, or allow myself to pass a mountain stream without drinking.

Along this Black Sea road in the autumn it would be impossible to starve, so lavish is Nature of her gifts. Here are many wild fruits, plums, pears, blackberries, walnuts, grapes, ripening in such superfluity that none value them. The peasant women pick what they need; the surplus is allowed to fall and rot into the soil.

I made my way to Ghilendzhik through miles of wild fruit-trees ranged in regular order. It is said that once upon a time when this territory belonged to Turkey, or even before then, the land was laid out in orchards and vineyards, and there was not a square foot uncultivated.

I ate of wild pears and kisil plums. The pears were more the concentrated idea of pears than that we take from gardens; the kisil plums, with which the bushes were flaming, are a cloudy, crimson fruit with blood-like juice, very tart, and consequently better cooked than raw. My dictionary tells me that the kisil is the burning bush of the Old Testament, but surely many shrubs claim that distinction.

It was a glorious walk over the waste from Kabardinka to Ghilendzhik, with all manner of beauty and interest along the way. I left the road and cut across country, following the telegraph poles. In front of me fat blue lizards scuttled away, looking like little lilac-coloured *dachshunds;* silent brown snakes shot out of reach at the sight of my shadow; and every now and then, poking and grubbing like a hedge-hog, behold a large tortoise out for prey like his brother reptiles. This domiciled the tortoise for me; otherwise I had only associated him with suburban gardens and the "Zoo." Now as he hissed at me angrily I knew him to be a lizard with a shell on his back. I picked up several of them and examined their faces—they didn't like that at all. They have a peculiar clerical appearance, something of the sternness and fixity of purpose which seems to express itself in the jaws and eyes of some learned divines.

With what eagerness the tortoises scrambled away when I disturbed them. They run almost speedily in their natural state. I was amused at the strength of their claws, and the rate at which they tore a passage into a thicket and disappeared.

Half-way to Ghilendzhik there is a stone quarry, and there one may see thousands of what are called in England "Cape gooseberries," bright berries of the size and colour of big ripe strawberries. They peeped out shyly everywhere among the tall grasses and the ground-scrub. Above them were stretches of saffron-coloured hollyhocks, a flood of colour, and with these as sisters, evening primroses, a great abundance. Lilac and crimson grasshoppers rushed over them, jumping into the air and into vision, a puff of bright colour—then subsiding into the greyness of the dust as they alighted and the sombre wing-cases closed over their little glory. On the ground when waiting to spring, these grasshoppers looked as if made of wood: they looked like displaced chessmen of ancient workmanship.

What a rush of insect life there was in the air, new-born fritillary butterflies like little flames, dragon-flies, bee-hawks, fat sun-beetles, gorgeous flies, the sinister green praying-mantis! The Athena of the air expressed herself in all her wonder.

Ghilendzhik is a collection of datchas (country-houses) and Caucasian dwelling-places. Its name signifies "The White Bride," and it is a quiet, beautiful watering-place in a pure bay, beloved of all Russians who have ever visited it. It is the healthiest resort on the whole Black Sea shore, continually freshened by cool breezes from the steppes. It is yet but a village, utterly undeveloped, unpavemented, without shops or trams or bathing-coaches, or a railway station, and those who visit it in the season regard themselves rather as a family party. The beach is private, and a bathing costume is rather a rarity. It is an amazing testimony to the simplicity of the Russian that the upper classes behave at the seaside with little more self-consciousness than the peasant children by the village stream. When Ghilendzhik is commercialised to a Russian Brighton it will be difficult to imagine what an Eden it once was.

I had looked forward to my arrival, for I had a Russian friend there, living for the summer in her own datcha, and I had received a very warm invitation to stay there some days.

The welcome was no less warm than the invitation. I arrived one evening all covered with dust, my face a great flush of red from the sun, my limbs agreeably tired. The house was a little white one on the very edge of the sea. Part of the verandah had lately been washed away in a storm, so close was the datcha to the waves. I went in, washed, clad myself in fresh linen—the road-stained clothes were taken away with a promise of return clean on the morrow—borrowed some slippers, and sitting in an easy-chair on the verandah, lounged happily and chatted with my hostess.

Varvara Ilinitchna is a Russian of the old type—you don't find many of them nowadays, most of her friends would add—simple, quickwitted, full of peasant lore, kind as one's own mother, hospitable as those are hospitable who believe from their hearts that all men are brothers.

I was introduced to all the neighbours, to the visitors and the natives, and of course invested with much importance as one who wrote books, had no fear, who even intended pilgrimaging to Jerusalem.

"You sleep under the open sky—that means you have outlived fear," said Varvara Ilinitchna with some innocence.

Our next-door neighbour was a beautiful Greek girl, a veritable Helen, for the sake of whose beauty one might give up all things. Young, elegant, serpentine; clad in a single garment, a light cinnamon gown clasped at the waist; no stockings, her legs bare and brown; on her head a Persian scarf embroidered with red and gold tinsel; her face white, with a delicate pink flush over it; hair and eyes black as night, but also with a glitter of stars. Wherever she walked she was a picture, and whether she was working about the house, or idling with a cigarette on the verandah, or running over the sand to spank mischievous boys who had been trespassing, she was delicately graceful, something to watch and to remember. I shall remember her chiefly in the setting of the night when the moon cast her lemon-coloured beams over the sea.

"Very beautiful and very young," said my hostess, "but already she has a history. She is only eighteen, but is married and has run away from her husband. She wanted to marry a Russian, but her family forced her to take for husband a Greek, an old man, and so jealous and so frightened of the effect of her beauty upon other men that he shut her up and made her wear a veil like a Turk. He would not let her out by herself, and he never brought any friends home; he took to beating her, and then she ran away. Her father received her and promised to protect her. The old Greek cannot get at her any more; he has given her up and gone away."

"Good for her! "I hazarded.

"Not at all good," was the answer. "She has a husband and yet has none. She is young, but she can't marry again because she has a husband already."

At Ghilendzhik all meals were served on the verandah, and one lived constantly in touch with the varying moods of the sea.

My hostess was a talker, ready to sit to any hour of the night chatting of her life and of Russia. It was very pleasant to listen to her. We sat together on the balcony after tea, with a big plate of grapes between us, and I heard all that the world had to say at Ghilendzhik.

A burning topic was the ruin that the sea had made of the verandah wall. "The sea has been gradually gaining on us," said my friend, "When we came here, the village Council reckoned on that. They smiled when we bought the house, for they held that in quite a short time it would be washed away. The Council wishes to build a fine esplanade all along the sea-front—our house stands in the way and they don't wish to buy us out. 'You'd better buy the datcha,' said Alexander Fed'otch to them, 'Oh no,' said they, 'we leave that to God'—by 'God' meaning the sea. They bound us under a contract not to build anything in front of the house: they said they did not wish the view to be obstructed, but in reality they did not want us to put up any protection against the waves. They left the rest to Providence. The result was that the whole property was nearly washed away in a storm.

"It happened like this. We were away at Vladikavkaz, and Vassily, the watchman, was living in the house with his wife and family, looking after it in our absence. There came a storm one evening. No one paid any attention at first, but it became so bad in the night that even Atheists were at their prayers. At three o'clock in the morning all the villagers were up and dressed and watching it. They were afraid, not only for our house, but for the rest of the village: no one remembered such a storm. As for our datcha, being as it is the nearest to the sea, the waves were already washing stones and mortar away. Vassily worked as hard as man could, shifting the furniture, taking out his household things, and trying to save the house. The villagers helped him—even the councillors who had hoped for the storm, they helped.

"The storm did not abate, so the priest was sent for, and he decided to hold a prayer service on the seashore and ask God to make peace on the water. They brought the Ikons and the banners from the church, took the Service in case of great storms or danger, and when they had sprinkled holy water on the waves, the storm drew to a lull and gradually died away. The datcha was saved; perhaps the whole village. *Slava Tebye Gospody!* Glory be to Thee, O God!

"They wrote to us at Vladikavkaz what had happened, and of course we came down quickly. Then what a to-do there was! We demanded the right to protect our property from the sea. The Council said, 'Yes, yes, yes, don't alarm yourself; you'll be quite safe, safe as the Kazbek mountain; we ourselves will protect you.' The Government engineer came round and said once more, 'Don't alarm yourself! We are going to build an embankment. Next year there will be a whole street in front of you, and electric trams going up and down perhaps.' "

"Did you believe him?" I asked.

"We didn't know what to do, believe him or disbelieve, but we knew he had been granted power to make investigations and draw up plans. For months, now, they have been measuring the depth of the water and testing this place and that. For my part, I think the preparations are only a device for making money. The engineer will enrich himself: the embankment and the street will be in his bank, but not here. The money they have spent already on his reports is appalling. But of course, if they *do* build an esplanade, our house will be worth three times what it cost us. We will let it as a café or a restaurant, and it will bring us rent all the year round. God grant it may be so!

"We resolved, however, to protect it, and we obtained permission to build a Chinese wall in front of it. But *Bozhe moi,* what that wall is costing us—already fifteen hundred roubles, and on the original estimate we thought five hundred.

"Even as it is we don't know how we stand. The engineer may claim that wall as belonging to the town. The town may have it knocked down, for it is built just outside our boundary line. We go down to the sand, and we have built upon the sand."

Obviously she hadn't built upon a rock.

"Now that they think of making a street in front of us, they will call part of the seashore land, and it will be surveyed. Some one will remark that we have encroached, and then down will go our wall and with it our fifteen hundred roubles."

I agreed with her and sympathised. The chances were certainly against the money having been profitably invested. But what an example of Russian ways!

We sat in silence and looked out over the placid waves on whose future kindliness so much of my hostess's happiness seemed to depend. It was a beautiful night. The sun had sunk through a cloud into the sea, and, as he disappeared, the waves all seemed to grow stiller and paler; they seemed full of anxious terror, as the faces of women whose husbands are just gone from their arms to the war. Dark curtains came down over their grief: the waves disappeared. The long bay was unruffled and grey to the horizon, like a sheet of unscored ice. Even the boats in the harbour seemed to be resting on something solid. The one felucca in front of us, with its five lines of rope and mast, grew darker and darker, till at last the moon rose and gleamed on her bows and cordage.

My hostess continued to talk to me of the fortunes of her property. "Twenty years ago," she said, "I was sitting on a log in a field one summer afternoon, when up comes an old peasant woman leaning on a stick and speaks to me in an ancient, squeaky voice:

" 'Good-day, **barinya**!'

" 'Good-day!' I said.

" 'Would you like to buy a little wooden hut and some land?'

" 'Eh, **Gospody**! What should I want with a little wooden hut?' said I. 'What do you ask for it?'

" 'Fifty roubles,' she squeaked. 'My son has written to me from Poltava. He says, "Sell the hut and come and live with me," so I'm just looking for a buyer.'

" 'What did you say?' I asked. 'Fifty roubles?'

" 'Fifty roubles, **barinya.** Is it too much?'

"I was astonished. A house and land for fifty roubles. Such a matter had to be inquired into. I felt I must go and look at the hut. I went and saw it. It was all right, a nice little white cottage and thirty or forty yards of garden to it. 'Here's your fifty roubles,' I said. And I bought it on the spot.

"We did nothing with it.

"Next summer, when I came down to Ghilendzhik, I said to my husband, 'Let us go and see our house and land.' Accordingly we went along to look. What was our astonishment to find it occupied by another old crone. I went up to the door and said:

" 'Good-day!'

" 'Good-day!' said a cracked old voice. And who might you be?'

" 'I might be the landlady,' I said. 'How is it you're here?'

" 'Oh, you're the **khosaika,** the hostess,' replied the old crone. 'Eh, dear! Eh, deary, deary! My respects to you. I didn't know you were the **khosaika.** I saw an empty cottage here one day; it didn't seem to belong to any one, so, as I hadn't one myself, I just came in.'

"The old dame bustled about apologetically.

" 'Never mind,' said I. 'Live on, live on.'

" 'Live on,' said Alexander Fed'otch.

"We went away and didn't come back to it or ask about it for seventeen years. Then one day I received a letter offering me twenty pounds (two hundred roubles) for the property, but as I had no need of money I paid no attention. A month later some one offered me thirty pounds. Obviously there was something in the air; there was some reason for the sudden lively interest in our property. Alexander Fed'otch went down, and he discovered that the site was wanted by the Government for a new vodka-shop. If we didn't sell, we should at last be forced to give up the property to the Government, and perhaps find ourselves involved in litigation over it. Alexander Fed'otch made negotiations, and sold it for ninety pounds—nine hundred roubles—think of it. And it only cost us five pounds to start with! Ah, here is a place where you can get rich if you only have a little capital."

"The old woman?" I queried. "Was she evicted?"

"Oh no, she had disappeared—died, I suppose."

"You made a handsome profit!"

"Yes, yes. But that's quite another history. You think we made eighty-five pounds profit. No, no. We ought to have invested the money quietly, but unfortunately Alexander Fed'otch, when he was selling the house, met another man who persuaded him to buy a plot of land higher up, and to build a grandiose villa upon it. They thought it a splendid idea, and Alexander Fed'otch paid the nine hundred roubles as part of the money down for the contractor. It was a great sorrow—for no profit ever came of it. It happened in the revolutionary time. We paid the contractor two thousand roubles, and then suddenly all his workmen went on strike. He was an honest man, and it was not his fault. His name was Gretchkin. He went to Novorossisk to try to get together a new band of men, and there he met with a calamity. He arrived on the day when the mutinous sailors were hanged, and the sight so upset him that he lost his head—he plunged into a barracks and began shooting at the officers with his revolver. He was arrested, tried, and condemned to death. The sentence, however, was commuted to penal servitude—that was when we got our Duma and there was the general pardon. Two thousand roubles were lost to us right away. The half-dug foundations of our house remained—a melancholy sight.

"The datcha is finished now; to-morrow you must go and see it. But it has cost us in all ten thousand roubles. I should be thankful to sell it for five thousand. Ai, ai, and we are growing old now and living through everything."

My hostess went out to fetch another plate of grapes.

"We wanted to put a vineyard round the datcha, but what with the children and the pigs mauling and biting at everything, it couldn't be managed. We had, however, a *pood* of grapes from one of our gardens this year."

The moon now bathed her yellow reflection in the mysterious sea, and we sat and looked at it together.

"Vasia, my son, who has taken his musical degree, will stay up all night to look at this sight," said my hostess. "It moves something in his soul."

It moved something in mine, and yet seemed strangely alien to the tale I was hearing. That moon had flung its mystery over an Eastern world, and it seemed an irrelevance beside the fortunes of a modern watering-place.

Varvara Ilinitchna went on to tell me of her early days, and how she and her husband had been poor. Alexander Fed'otch had taught in schools and received little money. Their two sons were never well. They had often wept over burdens too hard to bear.

One season, however, there came a change in their life and they became prosperous. They prayed to be rich, and God heard their prayer.

"We owe the change in our fortunes to a famous Ikon," said Varvara Ilinitchna. "It happened in this way. Alexander Fed'otch had an old friend who, after serving thirty years as a clerk in an office, suddenly gave up and took to the mountains. He was a wise man and knew much of life, and it was through his wisdom that we sent for the Ikon. We sheltered him all through the winters because he had no home, and he came to love us and enter into our life. He rejoiced with us on festivals when we were gay; when we were sad he sympathised. When we shed tears he shed tears also. One evening when we were more than ordinarily desperate he said to me, 'Take my advice; send for an Ikon of St. Spiridon of Tremifond.' The Ikon costs ten shillings, and ten shillings was much to us in those days. I told Alexander Fed'otch what our friend had said, and he, being a religious man, agreed. We sent ten shillings to Moscow and had the Ikon sent to us, and we took it to church and had it blessed.

"That happened in the autumn. Those were the days when the Vladikavkaz Railway was a novelty. The children, and even the grown-up people, did nothing but play at trains all day. We used to take in the children of the employees and look after them while their fathers and mothers were away. Well, in the following May a director of the railway called on Alexander Fed'otch and said he had a post to offer him.

" 'We are thinking of taking all the children of the railway employees, and establishing a school and *pension* for them where they can get good meals and be taught. We will provide you with a house and appointments, and you will get a good salary into the bargain. Your wife will be mother to our railway children, and you will be general manager of the establishment. Will you take the post?'

" 'With pleasure!' answered Alexander Fed'otch. But I for my part took some time to consider. It was hard enough to be mother to three children of my own. How could I be mother to fifty?

"However, we agreed to take the offer, and then suddenly we found ourselves rich and important people, and we remembered the Ikon of St. Spiridon of Tremifond and thanked God. If you are ever poor, if ever you want money, send for the Ikon of St. Spiridon. I advise you. Its virtues are famous."

"An evil Ikon, nevertheless, that Spiridon of Tremifond," I thought, but I wouldn't say so to my hostess.

"And you've been happy ever since?" I asked.

"Not happy. Who even hopes to be happy? But we did well. The railway company opened new establishments, and the directors have loved my husband, and one of them even said at a public meeting, 'Would to God there were more men in the world like Alexander Fed'otch!' We took larger charges and higher posts. We were even thanked publicly in the press for our services."

Varvara Ilinitchna sighed. Then she resumed her talking in a different tone.

"But we live through our fortune. Well, I understand it. It is our Karma after the Revolution. Property shall avail us nothing. Everything we have shall be taken from us. Look at this Chinese wall taking away all our money. Think of that foolish contractor Gretchkin and our costly datcha. Behold our sickly children. How much money have we not spent trying to heal our children, eh, eh! Doctors have all failed. Even a magic healer in the country failed."

"Tell me of him," I urged.

Varvara Ilinitchna went on only too gladly. She had found a listener.

"It was a peasant woman. She healed so many people that, though she was quite illiterate, the medical faculty gave her a certificate to the effect that she could cure. I know for a fact that when specialists gave their patients up as hopeless cases, they recommended her as a last resort. She was a miracle worker: she almost raised the dead. You must know, however, that she could only cure rheumatism cases. For other diseases there are other peasant women in various parts of Russia. We went to this one and lived a whole summer with her on a very dirty, dismal countryside. We were all bored to death, and we came away worse than we went. And all such things cost much, I assure you."

My hostess verily believed in the effect of the holy water on the stormy waves, in the gracious influence of St. Spiridon, and in the magical faculties of certain peasants. Yet observe she uses the word **Karma:** she calls herself a Theosophist. My long vagabondage she calls my **Karma.**

"My happiness," I corrected her.

"Happiness or unhappiness, it is -all the same, your **Karma.**"

She went on to talk of the great powers of Mme. Blavatsky, and she told me that Alexander Fed'otch had just ordered **The Secret Doctrine** to read. Good simple man, he will never get through a page of that abstruse work; and my hostess will understand nothing. Is it not strange—these people were peasants a generation ago; they are peasants now by their goodness, hospitality, religion, superstition, and yet they aspire to be eclectic philosophers? Varvara Ilinitchna has life itself to read, and she turns away to look at books. Life does not satisfy her—there are great empty places in it, and she would be bored often but that she has books to open in these places. She was very interesting to me as an example of the simple peasant mind under the influence of modern culture. Perhaps it is rather a shame to have put down all her old wife's talk in this way, for she is lovable as one's own mother.

VII

AT A FAIR

ONE misty morning in late October I arrived at Batum, pack on back, staff in hand, to all appearances a pilgrim or a tramp, and I drank tea at a farthing a glass in the fair.

"Pour it out full and running over," said a chance companion to the owner of the stall. "That's how we workmen like it; not half-full as for gentlefolk." The shopman, a silent and very dirty Turk, filled my glass and the saucer as well. And sipping tea and munching **bubliki,** we looked out upon all the sights of the **bazar.**

There lay around, in all the squalor that Turks love, the marvellous super-abundance of a southern harvest—spread on sacks in the mud—grapes purple and silver-green, pomegranates in rusty thousands, large dew-fed yellow apples, luscious dirt-bespattered pears, such fruits that in London even the rich might look at and sigh for, but pass by reflecting that with the taxes so high they could not afford them, but here sold by ragamuffins to ragamuffins for greasy coppers; and not only these fruits; but quinces and peaches, the large yellow Caucasian **khurma,** the little blood-red **kizil,** and many unnamed rarities. They all surged up out of the waste of overtrodden mire, as if the pageantry of some fairy world had been arrested as it was disappearing into the earth.

Then, beside these gorgeous fruits, in multitudinous attendance, a confused array of scarlet runners, tomatoes, cabbages, out-tumbled sacks of glazy purple aubergines, mysterious-looking gigantic pumpkins, buckets full of pyramidal maize-cobs, yellow, white-sheathed.

The motley crowd of vendors, clamouring, gesticulating, are chiefly distinguished by their hats—the Arabs in white turbans, the Turks in dingy fezes jauntily cocked over dark, unshaven faces, some fezes swathed in bright silk scarves; the Caucasians in golden fleece hats, bright yellow sheepskin busbies; the few Russians in battered peak caps, like porters' discarded head-gear; Persians in skull-caps; Armenians in shabby felts, astrakhans, or mud-coloured **bashliks.** The trousers of the Christians all very tight, the trousers of the Mahometans baggy, rainbow-coloured—it is a jealous point of difference in these parts that the Turk keeps four or five yards of spare material in the seat of his trousers.

What a din! what a clamour!

"Kopeika, kopeika, kopeika."

"Oko tre kopek, oko tre kopek, oko tre kopek."

Thus Christians shout against Mussulmans over the grape-heaps—one farthing, one farthing, one farthing; oko (three pounds) three farthings, oko three farthings, oko three farthings. Fancy shouting oneself hoarse to persuade passers-by to buy grapes at a farthing a pound!

My companion at the tea-stall, a tramp-workman from Central Russia, was astonished at the price of the grapes.

"It is possible to say that that is cheap," said he. "When I return to Russia I will take forty pounds of them and sell them in the train at twopence-halfpenny (ten *co-pecks*); that will pay for my ticket, I think, in the fourth class."

I watched the Turks trafficking, jingling their ancient rusty balances, manipulating their Turkish weights—the *oko* is not Russian—and giving what was probably the most marvellous short weight in Europe. The three-pound *oko* was often little more than a pound.

A native of Trebizond came and sat at our table. He wore carpet socks, and over them slippers with long toes curled upperward like certain specimens one may see in Bethnal Green Museum; on his head a straw-plaited, rusty fez swathed with green silk of the colour of a sun-beetle.

"The Italians have taken Tripoli," said the Russian, with a grin; "fancy letting those little people thump you so!"

"And the Japanese?" said a Caucasian quickly.

The Turk looked sulky.

"Italia will fall," said he. "She will fall yet, dishonourable country. They have stolen Tripoli. All you others look on and smile. But it is an injustice. We shall cut the throats of all the Italians in Turkey. Will you look on then and smile?"

A Greek sniggered. There were many Greeks at the fair—they all wear blue as the Turks all wear red.

When the Turk had gone, the Greek exclaimed:

"There's a people, these Turks, stupid, stupid as sheep; all they need are horns . . . and illiterate! When will that people wake up, eh?"

The Turks and the Greeks never cease to spit at one another, though the former can afford to feel dignified, victors of their wars with Greece. For the Italian the ordinary Turk has almost as much contempt as for the Greek. One said to me, as I thought, quite cleverly:

"A Greek is half an Italian, and the Italian is half a Frenchman, the Frenchman is half an Englishman, and you, my friend, are half a German. We have some respect for a German, for he is equal to a score of Greeks, a dozen Italians, or six Frenchmen, but we have no respect at all for the rest."

Twenty Arabs passed us at the stall—all pashas, a Georgian informed me. They had arrived the night before from Trebizond and the desert beyond. Their procession through the ragged market was something to wonder at—a long file of warriors all over six feet high, broad, erect, with full flowing cloaks from their shoulders to their ankles, under the cloaks rich embroidered garments. Their faces were white and wrinkled, proud with all the assurance of men who have never known what it is to stoop before the law and trade.

"They have come to make a journey through Russia," said the Georgian, "but their consul has turned them back. They will pray in the mosque and then return. It is inconvenient that they should go to Europe while there is the war."

A prowling gendarme in official blue and red came up to the stall and sniffed at the company. He pounced on me.

"Your letters of identification?" he asked.

I handed him a recommendation I had from the Governor of Archangel. He returned it with such deference that all the other customers stared. Archangel was three thousand miles away. Russian governors have long arms.

It is unpleasant, however, to be scrutinised and thought suspicious. I finished my tea and then returned to the crowd. There was yet more of the fair to see—the stalls of Caucasian wares, the silks, the guns, the knives, Armenian and Persian carpets, Turkish slippers, sandals, yards of brown pottery, where at each turn one sees huge pitchers and water-jugs and jars that might have held the forty thieves. At one booth harness is sold and high Turkish saddles, at another pannier baskets for mules. A flood of colour on the pavement of a covered way—a great disarray of little shrivelled lemons, with stalks in many cases, for they have been gathered hard by. In the centre of the market-place are all the meat and fish shops, and there one may see huge sturgeon and salmon brought from the fisheries of the Caspian. Garish notices inform in five languages that fresh caviare is received each day. Round about the butchers are sodden wooden stalls, labeled and there, wrapped in old rags, is much grey muddy snow melting and freezing itself. It has been brought on rickety lorries down the rutty tracks of the mountains, down, down into the lowland of Batum, where even October suns are hot.

Near the snow stalls behold veiled Turkish women just showing their noses out of bright rags, and tending the baking of chestnuts and maize cobs, sausages, pies, fish, and chickens. Here for eightpence one may buy a hot roast chicken in half a sheet of exercise-paper. The purchasers of hot chicken are many, and they take them away to open tables, where stand huge bottles of red wine and tubs of tomato-sauce. The fowl is pulled to bits limb by limb, and the customer dips, before each bite, his bone in the common sauce-bowl.

Those who are poorer buy hot maize cobs and cabbage pies; those who feel hot already themselves are fain to go to the ice and lemonade stall, and spend odd farthings there. I bought myself **matsoni,** Metchnikofs sour milk and sugar, at a halfpenny a mug.

The market square is vast. It is wonderful the number of scenes enacting themselves at the same time. All the morning in another quarter men were trying on old hats and overcoats, and having the most amazing haggling over articles which are sold in London streets for a pot of ferns or a china butter-dish. In another part popular pictures are spread out, oleographs showing the Garden of Eden, or the terror of the Flood, or the Last Judgment, and such like; in another is a wilderness of home-made bamboo furniture, a speciality of Batum. And for all no lack of customers.

What a place of mystery is a Russian Fair, be it in the capital or at the outposts of the Empire! There is nothing that may not be found there. One never knows what extraordinary or wonderful thing one may light upon there. Among old rusty fire-irons one finds an ancient sword offered as a poker; among the litter of holy and secular secondhand books, hand-painted missals of the earliest Russian times.

Nothing is ever thrown away; even rusty nails find their way to the **bazar.** The miscellanies of a stall might upon occasion be what is left behind after a house removal. On one table at Batum I observed two moth-eaten rusty fezes, a battered but unopened tin of herrings in tomato-sauce, another tin half-emptied, a guitar with one string, a good hammer, a door-mat worn to holes, the clearing of a book-case, an old saucepan, an old kerosene stove, a broken coffee-grinder, and a rusty spring mattress. Under the stall were two Persian greyhounds, also for sale. The shopmen ask outrageous prices, but do not expect to be paid them.

"How much the kerosinka?" I asked in sport.

"Ten shillings," said an old, sorrowful-looking Persian.

I laughed sarcastically, and was about to move away. The Persian was taking the oil-stove to bits to show me its inward perfection.

"Name your price," said he.

I did not want a kerosene stove, but for fun I tried him on a low figure—

"Sixpence," I said.

"Whew!" The Persian looked about him dreamily. Did he sleep, did he dream?

"You don't buy a machine for sixpence," said he. "I bought this second-hand for eight-and-sixpence. I can offer it to you for nine shillings as a favour."

"Oh no, sixpence; not a farthing more."

I walked away.

"Five shillings," cried the Persian—"four shillings."

"Ninepence," I replied, and moved farther away.

"Two shillings." He bawled something more, inaudibly, but I was already out of hearing. I happened to repass his stall accidentally later in the morning.

"That kerosinka," said the Persian—"take it; it is yours at one shilling and six-pence."

I felt so sorry for the unhappy hawker, but I could not possibly buy an oil-stove. I could not take one as a gift; but I looked through his old books and there found, in a tattered condition, *The Red Laughter,* by Leonid Andreef, a drama by Gorky, a long poem by Skitaletz, and a most interesting account of Chekhof's life by Kouprin, all of which I bought after a short haggle for fivepence, twenty copecks. I was the richer by my visit to his stall, for I found good reading for at least a week.

And the old Persian accepted the silver coin and dropped it into an old wooden box, looking the while with melancholy upon the unsold kerosinka.

VIII

A TURKISH COFFEE-HOUSE

IT sometimes happens that, entering a house, one enters not simply into the presence of a family but into that of a nation. So it was when I was received in a Little-Russian deacon's cottage in a village, on the Christmas Eve on which I first came to Russia. I came not to the deacon but to Russia itself, and when the Christmas musicians came and played before me it was not only Christmas music, or village music, that I heard, but the voice of a whole countryside and the song of a whole national soul. It sometimes happens that, looking at a picture, one sees not only its local and obvious beauty, but its eternal significance and message—that is a similar experience.

It happened to me whilst on a tramp in Trans-Caucasia to enter a coffee-house that was at once a Turkish coffee-house and Turkey itself. I lived for a whole night veritably in Turkey. In this way—

I came into a little town; it was a cold night and I wanted shelter. I entered a noisy Turkish coffee-house—there were at least a hundred such in the town—and asked if I might spend the night there. The owner, a young man in shirt-sleeves, very dirty and unshaven, and with an old fez on the side of his head, intimated that I might stay if I liked.

The café was a room full of poor Turks. Picture a crowd of ragged men, some in drab turbans with loose ends hanging down their backs, but most of them in dingy red fez hats, faces unshaved, mottled, ugly—a squat people, very talkative, but terribly mirthless; and in shadowy corners of the low dark café solitary persons with hook-nosed, ruminative faces. All about me was the din of the strange language, the clatter of dice and dominoes. All night long the doors of the café slammed and customers passed in and out, games were begun and played away, animated groups formed at certain tables and then broke up and gave way to new groups, loud discussions broke out over Turkish newspapers and politics and the war, in the course of which discussions the newspaper, a wilderness of Arabic, was often torn to bits—a series of scenes of tremendous animation and noise; but no one laughed.

In the clamour of tongues sounded again and again the name "Italia." The Turks were angry over the war, full of a restrained resentment and a profound need for revenge. It was a relief to me when one of them came to my table and talked to me in Russian.

"How goes the war?" I asked. "Is Italy losing?"

"Of course she is losing," he replied, lying sullenly; "and she must lose."

"But she has taken Tripoli and guards it with her navy. How can she lose?"

"The other Powers will make her disgorge it, or we will commence an endless hostility, not only against Italy and Italian trade, but against all whom we tolerate—the Western Christians."

A Caucasian, overhearing us, drew his forefinger along his throat from ear to ear, and smiled.

"There are more Mahometans than Christians," the Turk went on, "and they are strong men, heroes. The Italians are the worn-out scum of ancient Rome, getting the better of us ignobly. But they shall not spoil the Mahometan world. Not even the English, most powerful of the machine nations, shall overwhelm the true faith."

The keeper of the coffee-house came and stared at me. Two new customers came up, and I was pointed out as an Englishman. They talked about me in Turkish; other Turks came, they talked about England's rôle in the war, they scolded, gesticulated, poured forth endlessly, forgot me. Once more, though in a crowd, I was alone.

At this time a great diversion was caused. A blind musician came in. At midnight one would have thought no new development in the life of the café was likely to take place, but the musician brought into the room such a crush of people that on all sides I felt packed and crammed. A tall, gaunt man, hatless, shaggy-headed, his black locks falling over a strange yellow brow; eyes that saw not, looking through deep purple spectacles; and in his arms, like a baby, a long Armenian guitar—the musician was somewhat to wonder at. Hemmed in by the crowd, he yet found a little space in the body of the coffee-house, and danced to and fro with his songs like some strange being in a frenzy. He played with fire on his guitar, every minute breaking from his sparkling, thrilling accompaniment into a wild human chant, his face the while triumphant and passionate, but blind with such utter blindness that he seemed like the symbol of Man's life rather than a man; a great song of heart-yearning sung to the stars and to the Infinite rather than the singer of that song.

His fingers flowed over the long guitar; the wild words broke out; he flung himself in little zigzag steps to right, to left; the wild chant stopped; once more spoke only the strings. I looked at him and listened, and could not give myself enough to him.

At nearly two he made a collection and received many piastres and copecks, and the crowd who had listened to him began to disperse. At three o'clock the host signified that he wished to close the shop. To all the remaining customers Turkish delight was served out as a sort of parting gift. A dozen Turks, those who had homes, slunk away; the remainder, those who had no homes of their own, stayed to sleep.

The host now came to me and we did some business. I wanted to change some Turkish silver, as I was short of Russian money. As no bank would take this small coin I was obliged to try the coffee-house. Accordingly, I had asked my coffee-house keeper to buy a hundred or so piastres. After half an hour's haggling we struck a very bad bargain. I find the Turk more of a sharp than the Jew.

The long day was over. The shutters were pulled along in front of the shop and padlocked. A form was accorded me on which to sleep. Another form was drawn out into the middle of the room and placed at a certain angle, pointing to the East, I suppose. Then during half an hour the Turks ascended this form in turn, stood, bowed, knelt, prostrated themselves in silent prayer, reiteratedly. They prayed very differently from Russian peasants. Their movements were abrupt and mechanical, like steps in a military drill. They were nearer to spiritual death and praying-boxes than any I had ever watched pray before. I felt myself in the presence of a new form of piety. I had crossed the great broad line that separates Europe from Asia, and come to a place where Europe is not understood and therefore hated.

At six next morning the sleepers awoke and performed the same rites on the improvised praying-stool; the shutters were rolled back; the Turks who had homes returned; in came the Arabic newspaper; once more Turkish delight, coffee, the clatter of dice and dominoes, the gathering of animated groups, loud, unpleasant voices and mirthless vivacity—so the life of the coffee-house went on; so I imagine it goes on for ever.

As I think of this in retrospect it seems that the blind musician stood in some peculiar and significant relation to the more ordinary life about him. But for him, I should probably have omitted to describe my night among the Turks. He made the coffee-house worth living in, worth sketching, worth being re-seen in the reflection of words. He was what I should call the glory of the coffee-house.

Thus the garden of Eden was beautiful, but Adam and Eve in the garden were the glory of the garden, the highest significance of its beauty, the voice by which relatively dumb beauty got a step farther in expressing itself. The garden would never have been described but for the episode of Adam and Eve. It would not have been worth while to describe it. . . . The forest is beautiful, but the bird singing in the forest is the glory of the forest. The morning is beautiful, but the tramp walking in the morning is the glory of the morning; he also, in his youth and morning of life, is a voice by which beauty endeavours to reveal itself.

Each scene, each picture, has a highest significance if we could but find it. Thus the blind musician was a revelation of the very soul of the Turks. The tramp wandering through life and exploring it tries always to find what is particularly his in the scenes that come before his eyes. It is what he means by living a daily life in the presence of the Infinite.

IX

AT A GREAT MONASTERY

I

IN the Middle Ages, when Christianity was still young, there was much more hospitality than to-day. The crusader and the palmer needed no introduction to obtain entertainment at a strange man's house. The doors of castle or cottage, of monastery or cell, were always on the latch to the wanderer, and not only to those performing sacred dues but to the vagabond, the minstrel, the messenger, the tradesman, even to crabbed Isaac of York.

Since those days it has become clear that the thirty pieces of silver not only sold the author of Christianity but Christianity itself. As my Little-Russian deacon said, "Money has come between us and made us work more and love less. We are gathered together, not for love but for mutual profit. It is all the difference between conviviality and gregariousness." The deacon was right, and when one comes upon the Middle Ages, as yet untouched, in Russia, one reflects with a sigh—"The whole of Europe, even England, was like this once." One says with Arnold—

The Sea of Faith

Was once, too, at the full, and round earth's shore
Lay like the folds of a bright girdle furl'd.
But now I only hear
Its melancholy, long, withdrawing roar
Retreating to the breath
Of the night-wind, down the vast edges drear
And naked shingles of the world.

Day by day, as we live, we see the disintegration of that which Christianity means, the shattering of that brotherly love that makes, men nations and nations the children of God. Not without truth did Shylock say of his money that he made it breed. The pieces of silver have bred well; they jingle to-day in the pockets of millions of betrayers.

These thirty pieces did not pass out of currency, though the land that they bought was left desolate. They passed from hand to hand among the covetous throughout the first centuries of Christianity. The Jews clung to them as if they were life itself; but the early Christians, having something very much better than money to live for, coveted them not. And as long as the money remained with the Jews Christianity flourished. The two symbols opposed one another, and there was no question but that the Cross triumphed. Only when the Christians turned their backs on the Cross and hankered after the silver did the eternal nature of the betrayal manifest itself. When the Saracens began to be fought, not only by swords and faith but by the aid of Jewish money, and with the pomp and circumstance of war, then already Judas had been to the priests. When the knight or baron bequeathed the thirty Jewish pieces to the monastery Judas was already kissing the Master. When the hand that held the Cross loosened to take the silver, when the monks took the treasure of Earth and relinquished the treasure of Heaven, Jesus was already taken. It was but a short way to the crucifixion. The silver profiteth no man.

Where are the thirty pieces of silver now? Where are they not? When the rich holiday-maker comes scattering money in peaceful mountain valleys; when the peasant's son, infected by the idea of money, comes to town for his thirty shillings a week; when for the want of another thirty shillings he refuses to marry; when to save his mind some evangelical society—so called—accepts thirty shillings "charity"; when the millionaire leaves thirty thousand pounds to the hospitals to save his body; when a minister is paid three hundred pounds a year to save his soul; when a member of Parliament receives thirty pounds a month to remedy his social wrongs; when the love of the country girl he should have married is won by some rich man who thinks he can pay for it—on all these occasions and yet more, to examples innumerable, the curse of Judas shows itself, till every brick of our evil industrial cities is shown mortared round in bright silver hate.

As I write these lines one question is very urgent in the minds of Englishmen, that of the disestablishment and partial disendowment of a church. Once more the thirty pieces appear to be in the coffers of the church and they are attracting the curse. There is only one way for that church; it is to give up to the spoiler not only that which is demanded of it but all the material wealth it possesses, its endowments, estates, houses, palaces, sacred edifices; to lay down everything and be simply, for the moment, a church in the hand of God. As for disestablishment, the sooner Christians dissociate themselves from secular names and titles the better. The Christian church is one established for ever, upon a rock, and those who compose that church are they who love their neighbour as a brother.

We have hope of new life, otherwise it were folly to write at all. The great distress which the modern commercial life causes the individual soul is perhaps a blessing in disguise; it causes the individual to pause and think, causes him to rebel, to try and imagine a way to true salvation. For, despite Progress and the benefit our posterity is supposed to be going to derive from it, it is an undisguisable fact that life, the wonderful and strange gift given to the individual perhaps once in an eternity, is being used without profit, without pause, without wonder. We are like people who have lost their memories on the way to a feast, and our steps, in which is only dimly felt the remembrance of a purpose, take us nowhither. We loiter in musty waiting-rooms, are frustrated by mobs, and foiled by an eternal clamour. We have forgotten the feast and occupy ourselves in all manner of foolish and irrelevant ways. Only now and again, struck by the absurdity of our occupations, we grope after our lost consciousness and feel somehow that somewhere out beyond is our real destination, that somewhere out there a feast is proceeding, that a cover is laid for us and dishes served, that though we are absent the master calls a toast to us and sends messengers to find us.

The **somewhere-out-beyond** has for me been Russia. I do not suggest that it is Russia for every one. There are many tables at the feast, and the messenger sent after the absent must tell of those who sit at his own table. I think there is the same wine and the same fare at all tables. I tell of the hospitality of Russia, the hospitality of mind and of hand found amongst a simple people.

In October 1911 I arrived as a pilgrim at the monastery of Novy Afon, or, to translate the Russian into more recognisable terms, New Athos, and I obtained the hospitality of the monks.

There are three sorts of monasteries in Russia, one where there is great store of gold and precious stones as in Troitsky Lavra near Moscow, another where there are ancient relics and ikons of miraculous power as at Solovetz, and a third where there is neither the distinction of gold nor of relics, where the power of the monks lies in their living actual work and prayer. To the last-named category belongs Novy Afon.

It is very likely that the immense wealth of the other monasteries may invite the hand of the spoiler. Even now the monks are notorious for drunkenness and corruptibility: the institutions are moribund, and there is no doubt that if revolution had overturned the Tsardom the rich monasteries like the Troitsky would have been sacked. Perhaps even Novy Afon and many another spiritual mother would have shared a common fate with their depraved sisters. That is as may be. The Revolution did not succeed and could not, because the common peasantry still prayed in the temples which the Revolutionaries would have destroyed. The living church of Russia required its buildings even though the caretakers of these buildings were in some cases false stewards.

But there is no question of false stewards at Novy Afon. It is a place where a Luther might serve and feel no discontent, a place of new life. It looks into the future with eyes that see visions, and stretches forward to that future with hands that are creative; an institution with no past but only a present and an idea, not acting by precedent or tradition but taking its inspiration straight from life's sources.

II

It will be profitable to describe the monastery just as I saw it and felt it to be, on the occasion of my arrival there after five hundred miles tramping in the autumn of 1911. I had overtaken many pilgrims journeying thither, and the nearer I approached the more became their numbers. There were many on foot and many in carts and coaches. Multi-coloured diligences were packed with people and luggage—the people often more miscellaneously packed than the luggage, clinging on behind, squashed in the middle, sprawling on the top. The drivers looked superb though dressed in thousand-times-mended black coats, the post-boys tootled on their horns, and the passengers sang or shouted to the music of accordions. Of course not all those in the coaches were pilgrims religiously inclined; many were holiday seekers out for the day. The gates of Novy Afon are open to all, even to the Mahometan or the Pagan. It was a beautiful cloudless morning when I arrived at this most wonderful monastery in the Russian world—a cluster of white churches on a hill, a swarm of factories and workshops, cedar avenues, orchards, vineyards, and, above all, tree-covered mountains crowned by grey towers and ancient ruins, the whole looking out on the far sea.

At the monastery gates were a cluster of empty coaches waiting for passengers, the drivers sitting in the dusty roadway meanwhile, playing cards or eating chunks of red melon. Pilgrims with great bundles on their backs stood staring vacantly at the walls or at the sea; monks in long grey cloaks, square hats, and long hair, passed in and out like bees about a hive, and from a distance came a musical drone, the chanting of church services.

Pack on back, staff in hand, no one took me for other than a Russian pilgrim till

I showed my passport. I entered the monastery, asked one of the monks where to go, and was at once shown to a room, a little square whitewashed apartment with four hard couches; the room looked upon the hostelry yard, and was lit within by electric light—the monks' own manufacture. No one asked me any questions—they were too hospitable to do that. I was at once taken for granted as one might be by one's own family after returning home from a week-end in the country. When I had disposed my clothes, brushed away some of the dust, changed boots, and washed, the novice who had shown me my room tapped at the door and, looking in with a smile, told me I had come just in time for dinner. All along the many corridors I heard the tinkling of a dinner-bell and a scuttling of many feet.

The dinner was served in three halls: two of them were more exclusive apartments where those might go who did not care to rub shoulders with the common people; but the other was a large barn where any one who liked to come took the chances of his fellow-man, be he peasant or pilgrim. It was in the barn that I took my seat among a great crowd of folk at two long, narrow tables. Round about us on the walls were a multiplicity of brightly coloured ikons, pictures of the abbot, of Tsars, of miraculous happenings and last judgments. On the tables at regular intervals were large iron saucepans full of soup, platters of black bread, and flagons of red wine.

A notice on the wall informed that without prayer eating or drinking was forbidden, and I wondered what was going to happen; for although we had all helped ourselves in Russian fashion, no one had as yet said grace, and there was an air of waiting among the party. Suddenly a voice of command cried "Stand!" and we all stood like soldiers on drill. We all faced round to the ikons, and to a monk standing in front of them. A long prayer was said in a very military fashion, and then we all crossed ourselves and took our places at the tables once more. Five of the brethren were in attendance, and fluttered up and down, shifting the bread or refilling the wine bowls.

We were a mixed company—aged road-worn pilgrims, bright boys come from a local watering-place by coach, red-kerchiefed peasant women, pleasant citizens' wives in town-made blouses, Caucasians, a Turk, a Jew, an Austrian waiter, and many others that I took no stock of.

The diet is a fast one, just as the hard beds are penance beds, and no one can procure anything different at Novy Afon for any amount of money. Even in the hall reserved for dignitaries and officials the fare was the same as for us in the tiers état. The soup was of vegetables only, and much inferior to what the tramp makes for himself by the roadside. The second course was cold salt fish or boiled beans and mushrooms, and the third was dry maize-meal porridge. As each plate was put on the table the brother told us it came from God, and whispered a blessing.

There was not much talking; every one was busy eating and drinking. The wine was drunk plentifully, though without any toasts. One felt that more generosity was expressed in the provision of wine than in the other victuals. But for the meal only ten minutes and then once more the peremptory voice "Stand!" and we all listened to a long thank-offering and bowed before the ikons. Dinner was over.

Dinner was at eleven in the morning; tea with black bread and no butter at three; supper, a repetition of the dinner menu, at seven; and all doors closed and the people in their beds by eight-thirty. After many nights in the open I slept once more with a roof over my head, and looking up in the night, missed the stars and wondered where they were.

III

The monastery bells in pleasant liquid tones struck every quarter of an hour, and at two o'clock in the morning I was awakened by a great jangling, and the sound of steps along the stone corridors. I asked my companions—I was sharing my room with an Armenian and a Russian—what was the reason of the bell, and I learned that it was the call to early prayers. We none of us got up, but I resolved to go next night if it were possible.

Next day was one of relaxation after tramping. The Armenian went off ten miles to a celebrated cave and a point of view, "the swallows' nest"; he wished me to accompany him, but I had not come to Novy Afon to find points of view or the picturesque—moreover he had come by steamboat and was fresh, I had come on foot five hundred miles and wanted a rest.

In the morning I looked through the workshops, chatted with a master in the little monastery school, lounged in the orange groves and cedar avenues. After dinner, as I sat near the pier, a monk pointed out to me some artificial water where willows drooped, and white swans rode gracefully under them. "You ought to come here at *Kreschenie*—Twelfth-Night. We make of that water a little Jordan in memory of the Jordan where the Son of God was baptized. The ponds are all decorated with freshTcut grass, laurel leaves, and cypress branches, myrtle and oleander, many roses and wild flowers. Scarcely anywhere in all Russia could there be found such flowers at that time of the year."

"Have you pilgrims then?" I asked.

"Oh yes, many. They come from all the district round about, to dip themselves in the water after it has been made holy. We keep the festival very solemnly. The Archimandrite comes down from the monastery, and after him the priests, the monks, the lay brethren, the labourers, the banners and their bearers, and the sacred Ikons. There is a long service. Though the month is January, the weather is often bright and warm as early summer, and the mountains look very beautiful."

As we were thus talking, the Archimandrite, Ieronym himself, came out of the hostelry yard and passed us, a benign old man, devout and ancient of aspect, but kindly and wise. He is accounted a living saint, and it may well be that after his death he will be canonised. Novy Afon has only been in existence thirty years, and he has been abbot all the time. The monastery has been his own idea, it has grown with him. If Novy Afon is a fountain of life, he is the rock out of which the fountain springs. The whole monastery and all its ways are under his guidance, and as he wishes them to be. They are as a good book that he has written, and better than that.

He went to a gorgeous little chapel at the base of the landing-stage, there to hold a service in memory of the visit to New Athos of their highnesses the late Tsar, Alexander the Third, and his queen, on that day 1888. Presently behold the worthy abbot in his glorious robes, cloth of gold from head to foot, and on his head, instead of the sombre black hat of ordinary wear, a great golden crown sparkling with diamonds and rubies. The many clergy stood about him in the little temple, or beyond the door, for there was not room for all, with them some hundred monks, and the multifarious populace. The service was read in hollow, oracular tones, and every now and then a storm of glorious bass voices broke forth in response. Evidently the Ikon of the Virgin named *Izbavelnitsa* was being thanked for her protection of the Tsar in a storm. So much I could make out; and every now and then the crowd sang thanks to the Virgin. At the end of the service the Archimandrite, who had had his back to the people all the time—or rather, to put it more truly, had all the time looked the same way, *with* the people—turned, and lifting and lowering the gold cross which he held in his hands, gave blessing. The heads and bodies of the worshippers bowed as the Cross pointed toward them.

The service was over. As the abbot Ieronym resumed his ordinary attire, and left the temple, the hundred or so peasant men and women pressed around him, and fervently kissed his little old fingers, white and delicate. I watched the old man give his hand to them—I watched their eagerness. Religion was proved to be Love.

IV

What struck me particularly on entering Novy Afon was the new tone in the every day. There was less of the *barin* and servant, officer and soldier feeling, less noisy commanding and scoldings, even less beating of the patient horses that have to carry such heavy loads in Russia. Instead of these, a gentleness and graciousness, something of that which one finds in artistic and mystic communities in Russia, in art and in pictures, but which one seldom meets with in public life. Here at New Athos breathes a true Christianity. It was strange how even the undying curiosity of the Russian had been conquered; for here I was not asked the thousand and one impertinent questions that it is usually my lot to smile over and answer. There was even a restraint in asking me necessary questions lest they should be difficult to answer.

Then not one of the monks possesses any property of his own, even of a purely transitory kind, such as a bed or a suit of clothes. They have all in common, and they have not that nicety or necessity of privacy which would compel an English-man to claim the right to wear the same coat and trousers two days running. But the monks are even less diffident of claiming their own separate mugs and plates at table, and are unoffended by miscellaneous eating and drinking from one another's dishes.

Every one is the servant of all—and without hypocrisy—not only in act but in sentiment and prayer. Wherever I went I found the tone ring true.

This fair exterior glory seems to spring from a strong inner life. Religious life in the Holy Orthodox Church, with its many ordinances and its extraordinary prox-imity to everyday life, is not allowed to be monotonous and humdrum. Each day at New Athos is beautiful in itself, and if a monk's life were made into a book of such days one would not turn over two pages at once.

The day begins at midnight, when, to the occasional melancholy chime of the cathedral bell, the brothers move to the first service of the morning. On my second night at Afon I wakened at the prayer-bell and joined the monks at their service. In the sky was a faint glimmer of stars behind veiling clouds. The monastery, resplen-dent with marble and silver by day, was now meek and white in the dark bosom of the mountain, and shining like a candle. In the church which I entered there was but one dim light. The clergy, the monks, the faces in the ikon frames all were shad-ows, and from a distance came hollow shadow music, *gul-l-l,* the murmur of the sea upon the shore. It was the still night of the heart where the Dove yet broods over the waters and life is only just begun. At that service a day began, a small life.

When the service was over and we returned to our rooms, morning had advanced a small step; the stars were paler, one just made out the contours of the shadowy crags above us.

Just a little sleep and then time to rise and wash and breakfast. The monks in charge of the kitchen must be up some time before the rest of us. At 8 A.M. the morning service commences, and every monk must attend.

Then each man goes to his work, some to the carpentry sheds, others to the unfinished buildings, to the brickworks, the basket works, the cattle yards, the orchards and gardens, the cornfields, the laundries, leather works, forges, etc., etc., etc.; the teachers to the schools where the little Caucasian children are taught; the abbot to his cell, where he receives the brothers in turn, hears any confession they may wish to make, and gives advice in any sorrow that may have come upon any of them. The old abbot is greatly beloved, and the monks have children's hearts. Again in the evening the day is concluded in song and prayer. Such is the monastery day.

No doubt the upkeep of this great establishment costs much; it does not "pay"— the kingdom of God doesn't really "pay." Much money has to be sent yearly to Novy Afon . . . and yet probably not so very much. In any case, it is all purely administered, for there are no bribe takers at the monastery. For the rest, it must be remembered that they make their own clothes and tools, grow their own corn and fruits, and manufacture their own electric light. They have the means of independence.

Such monasteries as Novy Afon are true institutions of Christianity; they do more for the real welfare of a people than much else on which immense sums of money are spent. It is a matter of real charity and real hospitality both of hand and mind combined. The great monastery sits there among the hills like some immense mother for all the rude, rough-handed tribes that live about. In her love she sets an example. By her open-handedness she makes her guests her own children; they learn of her. Not only does she say with Christ her Master, "Suffer the little children to come unto Me, for of such is the kingdom of heaven," but she makes of all those who come to her, be they fierce of aspect or bearded like the pard, her own children. When the night-bell has rung and all are in their beds—the five hundred brethren, the many lay workers, the hundreds of guests gathered from all parts of Russia—the spirit of the monastery spreads itself out over all of them and keeps them all warm. The whole monastery is a home, and all those who are within are brothers and sisters.

V

Though Novy Afon is new, it is built upon an old site. There was a Christian church there in the second and third centuries, but it was destroyed by the Persian fire-worshippers; it was restored by the Emperor Justinian, but destroyed once more by the Turks. So completely did the Moslem take possession of the country that Christianity entirely lapsed till the Russian monks sailed down there two years before the Russo-Turkish war of 1877. Novy Afon is without Christian traditions. It takes its stand completely in the new, and is part of that Russian faith which has no past, but only a future. The third century ruins of the cathedral and the Roman battlements are indeed of great interest, and many people climb the two thousand feet high crag to look out from the ancient watch-tower. But the attitude of the monastery is well explained in the words of a monk:

"People come here to worship God, and we stand here as a witness of God, to pray continually for the coming of the Kingdom, and to succour those who come to us. It would be a sign of disrespect to our church if people came here merely to see the ancient remains."

I for my part, being of the old though also of the new, was eager to climb the steep stone way along which in ancient days had ridden crusaders and mediæval warriors. Great trees now grew through the rent wall of the cathedral, and slender birches grew straight up in the nave to the eternal roof which had supplanted that of time—to heaven itself. . . .

But alas for romance, the Russians are restoring the church, clearing away the old stones, chopping down the trees. An ikon has been set up within the old building, and the latter is already a place of worship. Once more: to the eye of a monk a ruined temple is somewhat of an insult to God. There is no fond antiquarianism; all the old Latin inscriptions and bas-reliefs that have been found have been mortared together at random into one wall; all the human bones that have been unearthed, and they are many, have been thrown unceremoniously into an open box. Even on the bare white ribs and ancient crumbling skulls, bourgeois visitors have written their twentieth-century names. Some ancient skeletons have been preserved in a case from pre-Mahometan times, and under them is written:

With love, we ask you, look upon us.
We were like you; you will be like us.

The recommendation is unavailing. The bones have been picked up, passed from hand to hand, scrawled upon, joked over. They are probably the remains of strong warriors and early Christians, and one can imagine with what peculiar sensations they, in their day, would have regarded this irreverence to their bones could they but have looked forward a thousand years or so.

It seemed to me, looking out from the watch-tower of Iver over the diminished monastery buildings and the vast and glorious sea, on that which must change and on that which in all ages remains ever the same, some reverence might have been begotten for that in the past which shows what we shall be in the future. The monks might have spared the bones and buried them; they might have left the ruins as they were.

I am told that in a few years the work of restoration will be completely achieved, services will be held regularly on the mountain top, and peasant pilgrims will gladly, if patiently, climb morning and evening up the stone way to the church, having no thoughts of any time but that in which they are worshipping. The Russian is racially young. He is in the morning and full of prophecy; only in the evening will his eye linger here in the emotions of romance.

Life at the monastery is new life; it is morning there—it is indeed only a little after the dawn. The day is as yet cool and sweet, and it gives many promises. We can see what the morning is like if we will journey thither.

III

I

THE BOY WHO NEVER GROWS OLD

UP to Christmas we are walking with the kings to the Babe's cradle, to the birth of new life and new hope. High in the heavens, and yet before us over the hard frost-bitten way, gleams the guiding star whose promise we divine. After Christmas we are walking with the spring, with a new, young, whispering child-life in the old heart. Though the winds be cold and snow sweep over the land, we know that winter and death are spent. Whilst the light grows stronger in the sky, something in us that is wooed by light responds. New eyes open in the soul. Spring comes, and then the tramp is marching with the summer. Down come the floods, and often for hours one takes shelter from the rain, and it seems as if all we hope for were being inundated. But, as I wrote before, "the spring is not advanced by rain, but it gathers strength in the rain to proceed more quickly when the sun comes out: so also with the tramp." Summer is the year itself, all that the other seasons have laboured for. It is the glory of the year. Then may the tramp cease marching, for in the height of summer nature also must cease, must cease from going forward to turn back. He may rest in the sun and mature his fruits. Autumn is coming and all the year's beauties must yield to death.

I think of my autumn on the way to Jerusalem, and all that a day told me then. The skies became grey at last, and cold searching winds stole into the summer weather. Many things that by sunlight I should have rejoiced in became sombre and ugly in the shade. The tobacco farms, with their myriad tobacco leaves drying and rotting from green into yellow, became ill-kept and untidy, the peasants harvesting them surly and unwashed: the sky spread over them no glamour.

I was walking over the swamps of Sukhum, and I noticed all that I disliked— the deep dust on the road, the broken-down bridges, the streams that cattle had befouled. It was perhaps a district that lacked charm even in fine weather.

There were some compensations. In a wilderness of wilted maize fields, and mud or wattle-built villages, one's eyes rested with affection upon slender trees laden with rosy pomegranates—the pomegranate on the branch is a lovely rusty-brown fruit, and the tree is like a briar with large berries. Then the ancient Drandsky Monastery was a fair sight, white-walled and green-roofed against the background of black mountains, the mountains in turn shown off against the snowy ranges of the interior Caucasus. The clouds hung unevenly over the climbing mountains, so that far snow-bestrewn headlands looked like the speckly backs of monsters stalking up into the sky.

I walked through miles and miles of brown bracken and rosy withered azalea leaves. There came a day of rain, and I spent thirty-six hours in a deserted house, staring most of the time at the continuous drench that poured from the sky. I made myself tea several times from the rainwater that rushed off the roof. I crouched over a log fire, and wondered where the summer had gone.

It needed but a day of rain to show how tired all nature was. The leaves that were weighed down with water failed to spring back when the rain had passed. The dry and dusty shrubs did not wash green as they do in the spring. All became yellower and browner. That which had come out of the earth took a long step back towards the earth again.

Tramping all day through a sodden forest, I also experienced the autumnal feeling, the promise of rest, a new gentleness. All things which have *lived* through the summer welcome the autumn, the twilight of the long hot day, the grey curtain pulled down over a drama which is played out

All day the leaves blew down as if the trees were preparing beds for the night of winter. In a month all the woods would be bare and stark, the bushes naked, the wild flowers lost in the copse; nought green but the evergreens. And yet but a week ago, rhododendrons at New Athos, wild roses and mallow in full bloom at Gudaout, acres of saffron hollyhocks, and evening primroses at Sotchi!

I had entered an exposed country, colder than much of the land that lay far to the north.

Two days later the clouds moved away, the zenith cleared, and after it the whole sky, and then along the west and the south, as far as eye could see, was a great snow-field, mountain after mountain, and slope after slope all white to the sky. A cold wind, as of January, blew keenly from the snow, and even froze the puddles on the road. It seemed we had journeyed thus suddenly not only to autumn, but to winter itself.

But at noon the sun was hot again. The new-born brimstone butterflies were upon the wing, a flutter of lambent green. They were of the time, and young. They must live all winter and waken every sunny day till next spring—the ambassadors of this summer to the next.

All that belongs to the past is tired, and even at the bidding of the sun insect life is loth to rise. The grasshopper is tired, the dragon-fly loves to crouch among the shadows, the summer-worsted fritillary butterflies pick themselves out of their resting-places to flutter a little further; their wings, once thick with yellow down and shapely, are now all broken, transparent, ragged.

The tramp's summer also is over. He will not lie full length in the sun till the spring comes round again. For the ground is wet, and the cold is searching. I walked more miles in the cold fortnight that took me to Batoum than in a whole month before New Athos. There was in the air a sting "that bids nor sit nor stand, but go."

Yet thoughts were plentiful, and many memories of past autumns came back to me. How many are the rich, melancholy afternoons of late October or early November, golden afternoons that occur year after year, when one feels one's thoughts parting from the mind easily and plentifully without urging, as overripe fruit falling at last since no one has grasped it before.

I hurried along the road, full of sad thoughts. The year was growing to be an old man. It looked back at spring, at the early days when it first felt the promises of life's glory and scarcely dared believe them true, at laughing May, at wide and spacious June, and then the turning of the year.

It almost seemed to me that I had grown old with the year, that I had even gathered in my fruits, as indeed I had, only they were more the year's fruits than mine: I had been the guest of the year.

I walked as within sight of a goal. In my imagination I saw ahead of me the winter stretches of country that I should come to, all white with snow, the trees all hoar, the people all frosted. I had literally become aware of the fact that I was travelling not only over land but over time. In the far horizon of the imagination I looked to the snowy landscapes of winter, and they lay across the road, hiding it, so that it seemed I should go no further.

Old age, old age; I was an old, bearded, heavy-going, wrinkled tramp, leaning on a stout stick; my grey hairs blew about my old red ears in wisps. I stopped all passers-by upon the road, and chuckled over old jokes or detained them with garrulity.

But no, not old; nor will the tramp ever be old, for he has in his bosom that by virtue of which, even in old age, he remains a boy. There is in him, like the spring buds among the withered leaves of autumn, one never-dying fountain of youth. He is the boy who never grows old.

Father Time, when he comes and takes some of us along his ways into middle-age, will have to pull. Time is a dotard, an aged parent; some boys that are very strong and young are almost too much for him; when he comes to take them from the garden of boyhood they kick and punch; when Time tries to coax them, pointing out the advantages of middle-age, they turn their heads from him and refuse to listen. If at last they are taken away by main force, it is with their backs to the future, and their faces all angry, twisted, agonised, looking back at the garden in which they want to stay.

II

THE STORY OF ZENOBIA

I HAVE known her in summer and in winter—in summer flushed and gorgeous like the wild rose, in winter lily-pale, or grey and haggard as the town she lived in. She was a beautiful daughter of the Earth, a wondrous flower. The summer night was in her dark hair, the south wind in her eyes. Whoever looked upon her in silence knew himself in the presence of the mystery of beauty, of the mystery of an imperious inner beauty. It was because of this, because of some majestic spirit manifest in her, shining through her in soul's colours, that I called her Zenobia, naming her after that Blythedale Zenobia who always wore the rich hot-house flower in her bosom. And it was to me as if my Zenobia wore that flower there also, and in silence, a new flower each day, wondrous and rich. Never could she be seen without that flower there, and it was as if on that flower depended her very life. Should the flower at any time be wanting, then all were wanting.

I remember her as she was one June when we gathered eglantine together, and the richest and deepest of all reds in roses. In the midsummer afternoons we plucked our garlands and brought them home at sunset time. Such afternoons they were, tempting all living things into the symphony of glory, such afternoons of splendour that now, looking back, it seems to be the very acme of their glory that we also were to be found there in those woods with all the rest. We came, soft stepping into the scene, and Nature, which moves continuously, harmoniously, did in the same moment build a throne and take us in it. At once the life from us flowed out, and the life about flowed in. Surely these were days of large orchestras, and of wonderful and complex melodies. Zenobia moved like a queen over the scene, her rich garments sweeping over the soft grass, her graceful arms swinging as with secret blessings. All the living things of the day seemed eager to be her pages; she was indeed a queen. The world needed her and the world went well because of her. The birds sang, they had not sung so sweetly but for her; the sun shone, it had not shone so brightly but for her; the roses stood on tiptoe on the bushes asking to be picked by her; the very air played lovingly about her, stealing and giving freshness.

The memory of all this comes out to me with a rush whenever I open a book of poems at a certain page, and with it comes the odour of sweet-brier and honeysuckle. It was in a June, one of the past Junes when we also were June glory, beautiful, full-blossoming, and not more self-conscious than the brier itself. I think now of the greens and crimsons, the blaze of holy living colour in which we were able to exist and breathe. . . . The afternoon passed, the evening came. Light unfolded silken banners of crimson floated down over the sky; crimson flower torches danced upwards from Zenobia's hands, living rose glowed from out her cheeks. About us and around floated lambent reds and blues and greens. The deep lake looked into her eyes, the trees nodded to her, birds flew over her, the first stars peeped at her.

Mysterious, breathless, was the summer night. An influence of the time seemed to press upon us; something exhaled from the mystery of flowers drew sleep down upon us. Twilight lay upon the eyebrows of the girl, and the cloud of her dark hair nodded over it like the oncoming night. We sat down upon a grass mound. We ourselves, Nature around us, all things of the day, seemed under a spell. Sleep lay about the roses, the bushes mused inwardly, the honeysuckle exhaled enchantment and was itself enchanted. Then the things of the night came. The myriad midges performed their rites over the blackthorn and the oak, and blackthorn and oak looked as if changed into stone. The mice and the shrews crept safely over the toes of the blackberry bushes, the rabbits came tumbling along through banks of inanimate grass. And fat night-moths sucked honey from half-conscious flowers, and the same moths whirred duskily round our gathered roses or darted daringly into our faces. We were like the flowers and the grass and the blackberry and blackthorn. The night which had overtaken them and put them to sleep had settled upon us also, and the things of the night came out securely at our feet. For a moment, a sport of habit had betrayed us to the old Eden habits, had taken us a step into a forgotten harmony. But below the surface the old fought secretly with the new, that old that seems so much the newest of the new, that new that really is so old and stale. The new must have won, and in me first, for I rose suddenly, brusquely, as if somehow I felt I had unawares been acting unaccountably foolishly. I looked at my companion; the mood was still upon her, and I believe she might easily have slumbered on into the night, but as she saw me rise, the new in her gained reinforcement, and she too rose in a sort of mild surprise. Now I think I might have left her there to awaken late in the night, a new Titania with the moonbeams coming through the forest branches to her.

I awakened her. I think she has often been awakened since then, but indeed it is seldom now that she is allowed to slip into such slumber. We walked home and I said some poems on the way; she heard. I think she heard in the same way as a flower feels the touch of a bee. No words had she, no poetry of words to give back. She had not awakened to articulateness. She had no thoughts; she breathed out beauty. She understood no thoughts; she breathed in beauty from around.

This was Zenobia, this was her aspect when she was taken, when the change came over her life.

That marvellous mechanism, the modern state, with its mysterious springs and subterranean attractions and exigencies, drew her in to itself. The modern state, whose every agent is called Necessity, had appealed to her. And she had been taken. She settled on the outskirts of a city and half her life was spent under a canopy of smoke, whilst in the other half she courted morning and evening twilights. In the first June of this time, in afternoons and evenings, we had lived together among the roses, and she had stood at the zenith of her glory. But with the coming on of autumn the roses withered, and something of the old dreaminess left her eyes. A little melancholy settled upon her, and she discovered she was lonely. But the town had seen her, and henceforth the town took charge of her. It sent its angels to her. One might wonder what the town used her for, this inarticulate one—it made her a teacher because of her good memory. Then it regarded her as "good material." It sent its angels, those voluntary servants of the state, the acquaintances who call themselves friends. These at first approved of her, always misunderstood her, and at length despised her. They misunderstood her, because a person truly inarticulate was incomprehensible to them. Her naïveté they mistook for insolence, her dreaminess for disrespect. They confused her memory with her understanding. They gave her books to read, brought her to lectures, sat her at the theatre, took her to hear sermons, prayed with her and drank with her the holy wine. And some would say, "Isn't she coming on?" or "Isn't she developing?" and others, more perceiving, would say, "Well, even if she isn't getting anything from it, at least she's seeing life"; while others, more perceiving still, gave her up as past hope. "She has no brains," they said. Others, still more perceiving, said she had no soul, no love; she cared for no one, understood nothing. She, for her part, went on almost as ever, and remained next to inarticulate. Only now and again the hubbub of battle in the schoolroom would awaken her to some sort of conscious exasperation. She would appeal to her class, staring at them with eyes from which all gentleness and affection had merged into astonishment and indignation. For the rest, lack of life, lack of sun, lack of life influence told upon her beauty. She did not understand the influence of the ill-constituted around her, and did not understand the pain which now and again thrilled through her being, provoking sighs and word-sighs. Then those friend-acquaintances, ever on the alert for an expression of real meaning, interpreted her sighs and longings for week-ends in the country.

Verily it is true, one cannot serve God and mammon. There was no health forthcoming through this compromise with life. She merely felt more pain. She continued her work in the town, and was enrolled and fixed in many little circles where little wheels moved greater wheels in the great state-machine. Ostensibly, always now, whatever new she did was a step toward saving her soul. I met her one January night; she was going to a tea-meeting in connection with a literary society. Very grey her face looked. Many of the old beautiful curves were gone, and mysteries about her dimples and black hair-clusters seemed departed irrevocably. Still much in her slept safe, untouched as ever, and, as ever, she was without thoughts. Her memory suggested what she should say to me. "It will be interesting," she remembered. I helped her off with coat and furs. She was dressed wonderfully. The gown she wore—of deep cinnamon and gold—was still the dress of Zenobia, and at her bosom the strange flower exhaled its mystery. I went in with her to the hot room. She was evidently a queen here, as in the forest glades. And her pale face lit up as she moved about among the "little-worldlings" and exchanged small-talk and cakes and tea. She was evidently in some way responsible for the entertainment, for the chairman said "they all owed her so much." I watched her face, it showed no sign of unusual gratification; had he slighted her, I am sure she would have listened as equably. What a mask her face was! The look of graciousness was permanent, and probably only to me did she betray her continuous sleepiness and lack of interest in the whole affair. Members propounded stupendously solemn questions about the "salvation of man," the "state of progress," the mystic meaning of passages of the Bible, and the like; and I watched her draw on her memory for answers. She was never at a loss, and her interlocutors went away, and named their little child-thoughts after her.

I took her away at last and whispered some things in her ears, and showed her what could be seen of moon and stars from the narrow street, and something of the old summer feeling came over us. How the old time sang sorrowfully back, plaintively, piteously. Our steps sounded along some silent streets, the doors of the little houses were shut and dark. They might have been the under doors of tombs. Silently we walked along together, and life sang its little song to us from the depths of its prison. It sounded like the voice of a lover now lost for ever, one worth more beyond compare than any that could come after.

There is no going back. I saw her to her little home and touched her tenderly at Goodbye.

She went in. The door closed and I was left standing alone in front of the closed door, and there was none around but myself. Then I was aware of a gust in the night-breeze blowing up for rain. Time had changed. Something had been taken from the future and something had been added to the past. The spiral gusts lifted the unseen litter of the street, and with them the harpies rose in my breast. And words impetuous would have burst out like the torrents of rain which the dark sky threatened.

The torrent came.

A girl like this simply grows like a flower on a heath, blossoms, fades, withers, and is lost. No more than that. I scarcely tell what I want to say. Oh, how strongly I would whisper it into the inmost heart! Life is not thoughts, is not calm, is not sights, is not reading or music, is not the refinement of the senses,—Life is—life. This is the great secret. This is the original truth, and if we had never begun to think, we should never have lost our instinctive knowledge. In one place flowers rot and die; in another, bloom and live. The truth is that in this city they rot and die. This is not a suitable place for a strong life; men and women here are too close together, there is not enough room for them, they just spring up thinly and miserably, and can reach no maturity, and therefore wither away. All around are the ill-constituted, the decaying, the dying. What chance had fresh life coming into the tainted air of this stricken city—this city where provision is made only for the unhealthy? For here, because something is the matter, every one has begun conscience-dissecting—thinking—and a rumour has got abroad that we live to get thoughts of God. And because thoughts of God are novel and comforting, they have been raised up as the great desideratum. And the state of society responsible for the production of these thoughts is considered blessed. The work of intensifying the characteristics of that society is thought blessed, and because in ease we think not, we prefer to live in disease. And the progress of disease we call Progress. So Progress and Thought are substituted for Life.

There *is* a purpose of God in this city, but there is as much purpose in the desert. There is no astonishingly great purpose. The disease will work itself out. And I know God's whole truth to man was revealed long since, and any one of calm soul may know it. The hope of learning the purpose through the ages, the following of the gleam, is the preoccupation of the insane.

What do all these people and this black city want to make of *her*? She, and ten thousand like her, need life. Life, not thought, or progress, just the same old human life that has always been going on.

The rain was pouring heavily and I took shelter. I felt calmer; I had unpacked myself of words. Rather mournfully I now looked out into the night, and, as it were, ceased to speak to it, and became a listener. A song of sorrow came from the city, the wailing of mothers uncomforted, of children orphaned, uncared for, of forsaken ones. I heard again the old reproach of the children sitting in the market. "Here surely," I said, "where so many are gathered together, there is more solitude and lonely grief than in all the wide places of the earth!" Voices came up to me from thousands in a city where thousands of hands were uplifted to take a cup of comfort that cannot be vouchsafed.

Is there a way out for *her*? Is there a way out for them? "For her perhaps, for them not," something whispered within me inexorably. "And Death?" The wind caught up the whisper "death" caressingly and took it away from me over the city, and wove it in and out through all the streets and all the dark lanes, and about the little chimneys, and the windows."

Is there a way out for her?—Perhaps. There are some beings so full of life that even the glutton Death must disgorge them.

III

THE LITTLE DEAD CHILD

IN the little town of Gagri on the Caucasian shore of the Black Sea there is a beautiful and wonderful church surviving from the sixth century, a work of pristine Christianity. It is but the size of a cottage, and just the shape of a child's Noah's Ark, but made of great rough-hewn blocks of grey stone. One comes upon the building unexpectedly. After looking at Gagri's ancient ruins, her fortresses, her wall built by Mithridates, one sees suddenly in a shadowy close six sorrowful little cypresses standing absolutely still—like heavily dressed guardsmen—and behind the cypresses and their dark green brooms, the grey wall of the church, solid, eternal. One's eyes rest upon it as upon a perfect resting-place. If Gagri has an organic life, this church must be its beating heart.

I came to Gagri one Saturday afternoon after the first two hundred and fifty miles tramping of my pilgrimage to Jerusalem, and at this little church I witnessed a strange sight. I had hardly admired the grey interior, the bare walls growing into the roof in unbroken curves, the massive stone rood-screen, the sorrowful faces in the holy pictures, when a little procession filed into the church; four girls carrying a flower-bedecked coffin, half a dozen elders, and a pack of children carrying candles—a sight at once terrible and diurnal, a child's funeral.

Russian churches, having no chairs, have the appearance of being almost empty. In the centre of this emptiness at Gagri church two trestles were put up, and the open coffin placed upon them; in the coffin, lying in a bed of fresh flowers and dressed in delicate white garments, was a little dead child. The coffin was perfectly and even marvellously arranged; it would be difficult to imagine anything more beautiful, and at the same time more terrible.

A girl of about four years, she lay in the coffin as in bed, with her head somewhat raised, and the face looking directly at the altar and at the sorrowful pictures; on her head was a cream silk embroidered bonnet, on her forehead, from ear to ear, a paper *riza* with delicate line drawings of the story of the girl's angel, St. Olga. A high lighted candle stood at her head, two little ones at each side, and two at her feet. The bonnet and the dress were tied with little bits of pink ribbon; the child's hands, small, white, all lovely, lay one upon another and in one of them was a little white cross. The face and arms were the colour of fine grey wax, the lips thin, dark red and set—the little dead girl looked steadfastly at the Ikons.

I stood and wondered. Round about the coffin were a score of people, mostly little children, who every now and then flicked away flies that were about to settle on the dead body. The grey church and its beauty melted away. There was only a little grey wax figure lying poised before the face of Christ, and little children flicking away flies.

Among the flowers in the coffin I noticed a heavy metal cross—it would be buried with her. Hanging over the trestles at each of the four corners were gorgeous hand-embroidered towels. "This is some rich person's child," I thought as I waited—it was twenty minutes before the father, the mother, and the priest arrived. I was mistaken; this was the child of ordinary peasants.

I wonder the mother was allowed to come to church; she was frantic with grief. When she came into the church she fell down on her knees and hugged the dead body and kissed it and sobbed—sobbed so horribly that except for the children there was no one present who kept dry eyes. The husband stood with his hands dangling at his side, his lips all puckered, his hair awry, and the tears streaming down his red cheeks.

But when the priest came in he took the good woman aside and quieted her, and in his words surely was comfort. "Those who die as children are assured of that glorious life above, for of them Christ said, 'Suffer the little children to come unto Me, and forbid them not, *for of such is the kingdom of heaven.'* Least of all should we grieve when a child dies."

I held a candle with the others and joined in the little service, and when the service was over ate of the boiled rice and grapes that were handed round to save us from evil spirits.

The candles were put out, the priest retired, and then the sobbing broke forth once more, the people crowded round the coffin and one by one kissed the little dead one, kissed her again and again. Most of all the little children kissed her, and the father in distraction stood by, calling out in broken treble, "Say good-bye to her, children, say good-bye!"

Last of all, the wild mother said good-bye, and was only taken away by sheer force. Then the lid was put on the coffin, and the four girls—they were each about twelve years old—lifted it on the embroidered towels and carried it out of the church.

The mother fainted and was taken into the open air, where one woman helped to revive her by pouring water on her head out of an old kettle, and another by drinking water and spurting it out again in her face. Meanwhile the father took eight nails—he had them in his pocket—and with all the crowd looking on, he nailed down the lid of the coffin. The girls once more lifted their burden upon the beautiful towels, and they bore it away to the grave. The crowd followed them with hymns—

All we like dust go down into the grave,

the sound of their singing almost drowned by the beating of their uneven steps. The music modulated and died away to the silence of the evening. The little church remained grey and ancient, and the six cypresses stood unmoved, unmoving, like guards before some sacred portal. . . .

And the pilgrim goes on his way.

IV

HOW THE OLD PILGRIM REACHED BETHLEHEM

AT New Athos monastery in one of the common hostels there were some hundred peasant men and women, mostly pilgrims. It was after supper; some of the company were melting away to the dormitories, others remained talking.

There was one topic of conversation common to all. An old greybeard palmer had broken down that afternoon and died. He had been almost his whole life on the road to Jerusalem, and we all felt sad to think that he had been cut off when he was truly nearing the Holy Land.

"He wished to go since he was a little boy," said old Jeremy, an aged pilgrim in a faded crimson shirt. Every one paid respect to Jeremy and listened to him. He was a placid greybeard who had spent all his life upon the road, full of wisdom, gentle as a little child, and very frail.

"He wished to go when he was a little boy—that means he began to go when he was a little boy, for whenever you begin to wish you begin the pilgrimage. After that, no matter where you are, you are sure to be on the way. Up in the north the rivers flow under the earth, and no one sees them. But suddenly the river appears above the land, and the people cry out, 'See, the river is flowing to the sea.' But it began to go to the sea long ago. So it was with Mikhail. All his life he was a pilgrim. He lived in a distant land. He was born of poor parents, not here, but far away in the Petchora province—oh, far, far away."

Grandfather Jeremy waved his hand to signify how far.

"Four thousand versts at least, and he hasn't come straight by a long way. Most of the way he walked, and sometimes he got a lift, sometimes a big lift that took him on a long way."

"Ah, ah!" said a youngster sympathetically, "and all in vain, all in vain—*naprasno, naprasno*"

Jeremy paid no attention.

"Big lifts," his voice quavered. "And now he is there. Yes, now he is there."

"Where, grandfather?"

"There, where he wished to be, in the Holy City. He had got very tired, and God had mercy on him. God gave him his last lift. He is there now, long before us."

"I don't see how you make that out," said a young man, a visitor, not a pilgrim. "God, I reckon, cheated him."

"God never cheats," said Jeremy calmly.

"God . . ." said the visitor, and was about to raise a discussion and try to convert these pilgrims from their superstition. But Jeremy interrupted him. For the old man, though a peasant had a singular dignity.

"Hush! Pronounce not His name lightly. I will tell you a story."

"Silence now!" cried several. "Hear grandfather's story!"

The old man then told the story of an aged pilgrim who had died on his way to Jerusalem. I thought he was repeating the story of the life of Mikhail, so like were his present words to those that had gone before. But the issue was different. In this case the pilgrim died and was buried in a little village near Odessa.

He was a penniless beggar. In grandfather's picturesque language, "he had no money; instead of which he bore the reproach of Christ. He found other men's charity. . . .

"All his life he wandered towards Bethlehem. He used to say he pilgrimaged not towards Calvary, but towards Bethlehem. The thought that the Roman officials had treated Christ as a thief was too much for him to bear.

"He who possessed all things they treated as one who had stolen a little thing. . . ."

The old man paused at this digression, and stared around him with an expression of terror and stupefaction.

There was a silence.

"Go on, Jeremy," said some one impatiently.

Jeremy proceeded.

"He always journeyed towards Bethlehem, and whenever he saw a little child, a little baby, he would say to the mother that it fore-told him what it would be like for him at the Holy Land. And of the cradles he would always say they were just the shape of the manger where the baby Christ was laid.

"He was very dear to mothers, you may be sure, and he never lacked their blessing.

"He travelled very slowly, for in Moscow a motor-car ran over his foot, and he always needed a strong staff. He was ill-treated sometimes in the towns, where the dogs bit him and the street children aimed stones. But he never took offence. He smiled, and thought how little his sufferings had been compared with those of the saints.

"So he grew old.

" 'You are old, grandfather; you will never reach Jerusalem,' the peasant women told him. But he always smiled and said, 'As God wills. Perhaps if I die I shall see it sooner.'

"And he died, poor, wretched, uncared for, in the streets of a little village near Odessa, and children came and beat off the hungry dogs from his body with sticks.

" 'What is this?' said one policeman to another.

" 'A ***Bogo-moletz*** (God-prayer) dead, that's all,' was the reply.

" 'No money?'

" 'None. If he had any his pockets have been picked.'

"By his passport he belonged to Petchora province, far away. No one knew him. No one claimed him.

" 'It means he must be buried at the public expense,' said the head man of the village, and spat upon the ground.

"In the whole village only the coffin maker rejoiced, and he had small cause, since a pauper's coffin costs but a shilling.

" 'He must be buried on the common,' said the head man. 'There's no room in the churchyard.'

" 'But a pilgrim,' said an objector. 'You must bury him in consecrated ground; you can't shut him out of the Heavenly Kingdom.'

" 'No matter. Ask the priest. If the dead man can pay for a plot of ground for a grave, well and good; or if the villagers will subscribe. . . .'

"The head man looked at the little crowd assembled. They were a poor and needy crowd. No one answered him. Then, without doing any more, the head man walked away, and the dead body remained in the street.

"It seemed no one would pay for the grave, but in the afternoon a woman who lived on the outskirts came and claimed the pilgrim as a distant relative. He could scarcely have been a relative, except inasmuch as we are all descended from Adam.

"The head man and the village priest rejoiced, and the woman took the dead body home and washed it, and clothed it in white linen, and she ordered a three-rouble coffin covered with purple cloth.

"But she was a very poor woman, and when she had paid for the grave she had no money to pay for singers and for prayers.

" 'God will have mercy', she said. 'And belike he was a good man, a pilgrim.'

"And that woman was a virgin," added Jeremy abruptly and, as I thought, irrelevantly. But the chambers of that old man's mind were strangely furnished.

"She was a virgin. What remains to be said? She hired a man to dig a grave, and another to wheel the barrow with the coffin. She had no friends who would follow the coffin with her, but in the main street she found a cripple whom she had once befriended, and two little boys who liked to sing the funeral chant.

"Thus the old pilgrim was taken to the grave, and in his honour a simple woman, two street children, and a cripple followed his corse."

There was a long pause.

"You think he died," old Jeremy went on. "Oh, no; he did not die, he only went on more quickly. When he fell down dead in the street his soul suddenly began a new life, a life like a dream. Whilst the dogs were barking and snapping at his old legs he suddenly saw in front of him in the darkness a great bright star beckoning him, and in his new life he got up from the road and rushed towards that star—rushed, for he felt young again, younger than any boy, and all the lameness and tiredness were passed away.

"Suddenly, in front of him, and coming to meet him, he saw a horse, draped all in silk, and attendants. A man came up to him and saluted him, offered him a crown, and bade him rise up upon the horse. He sat upon the horse, and, looking at himself, saw that he was dressed in cloth of gold. Behind him was a great train of attendants, carrying gifts. And they all journeyed forward, towards the star.

"Eh, brothers," said Jeremy, looking round, "what a change in the estate of our poor friend! He has now become one of the first, because on earth he was one of the last. He is a king."

The listeners were all silent, and the narrator enjoyed a triumph.

Jeremy's cracked old voice went on, and now again somewhat irrelevantly. "And the woman, who was a virgin, conceived and bore a child, and she was so poor that the child was laid in a manger. And three kings arrived, bearing precious gifts, and they did homage unto the child. It was at Bethlehem. One of these kings was the poor pilgrim who died on his way to the Holy Land."

"What woman was this?" said the visitor contemptuously. "Your wits are wandering, old man. Do you mean it was the same woman who buried him? "

"The same", said Jeremy huskily, "only in a different world. There are other worlds, you know. But it is very true. He came as one of the kings. And the woman now has a beautiful child. She knows. . . . So we shan't be very sad about Mikhail. I think he also to-day is following that star, and will be at Bethlehem to-night."

"Only it doesn't happen to be Christmas Eve," said the sceptical visitor.

"Eh, hey," said another pilgrim, breaking in, "there's a man—he doesn't know that it is Christmas every day in the year at Bethlehem."

IV

THE WANDERER'S STORY

I. MY COMPANION

WHEN star passes star once in a thousand years, or perhaps once in the forever, and does not meet again, what a tale has each to tell! So with tramps and wanderers when two meet upon the road, what a tale of life is due from one to the other. Many tramps have I met in the world. Far from the West I have met those who came far from the East, and men have passed me coming from the South, and men from the North. And sometimes men have suddenly appeared on my way as if they had fallen from the sky, or as if they had started up out of the earth.

One morning when I was dwelling in a cave between a mountain and a river I met him who tells this story. Probably the reader has never lived in a cave and does not appreciate cave life—the crawling in at night, the long and gentle sleep on the soft grey sand, the crawling out again at morning, the washing in the river, the stick-collecting and kettle-boiling, the berry-gathering, the lazy hours of noon, the lying outstretched on the springy turf, sun-drinking, the wading in the river and the plashing of the rushing water over one's legs; sunny days, grey days, rainy days, the joyous delight in the beautiful world, the exploration of one's own heart, the sadness of self-absorption.

It was on a grey day when I met the strange tramp whose life-mystery is here told. I came upon him on a quiet forenoon, and was surprised by him. He came, as it were, out of thin air. I had been looking at the river with eyes that saw not—I was exploring my own heart and its memories—when suddenly I turned round and saw him, smiling, with a greeting on his countenance.

It was long since I had looked upon a man; for though quite near the highway, no one had found me out in my snug cave. I was like a bird that had built a nest within earshot of a road along which many schoolboys ran. And any one discovering my little house was like to say, "Fancy, so near to the road, so unsuspected!"

"Good - morning, friend," said I, "and greeting! You are the first who has found his way to this cave. You are a wanderer like myself, I perceive. Come, then, and share my noonday solitude, and in return give me what you have to share."

"Forgive me," said he, "I thought I heard a voice; that was why I came. I thought I heard a call, a cry."

I looked at him. He was a strange man, but with something peculiarly familiar in his figure. His dark hair spread over a brow whiter than mine, and veiled two deep and gentle eyes; and his sun-tanned face and dusty hat made him look like a face such as one sometimes sees in a dream.

"You heard not me," I answered, "unless it was my thoughts that you heard."

He smiled. I felt we need not say more. I sat with my back to the sun and he lay stretched in front of me, and thus we conversed; thus two wanderers conversed, two like spirits whose paths had crossed.

"Now tell me," said I, "who you are, dear wanderer, stretched out at my feet like a shadow, and like a shadow of my own life. How long have you been upon the road, when did you set out, where is your home and why did you leave it?"

The tramp smiled.

"I am a wanderer and a seeker," he replied. "In one sense the whole world is my home, in that I know all its roads and am nowhere a stranger. In another sense I have no home, for I know not where I began or where I come from. I do not belong to this world."

"What!" said I, starting up suddenly and consequently disturbing my companion. "You are then an apparition, a dream-face, a shadow. You came out of thin air!"

I stood up, and he turned familiarly about me and whispered like an echo in my ear, "Out of thin air." And he laughed.

"And you?" he went on. "On what star did you begin? Can *you* tell me? Never yet have I found a man who could answer that question. But we do not know, because we cannot remember. My conscious life began one evening long ago when I stepped out of a coach on to a high road, this same road by which you have your cave. I had come from God-knows-where. I went backward, I came forward; I went all about and round about, and never found my kith and kin. I was absorbed into the world of men and shared its illusions, lived in cities, worked for causes, worshipped idols. But thanks to the bright wise sun I always escaped from those 'gloomy agreeable nooks.' It has now become my religion to avoid the town, the places where men make little homes which make us forget that in truth we have no homes. I have learned to do without the town, without the great machine that provides man with a *living.* I have sucked in a thousand rains, and absorbed a thousand suns, lain on many thousand banks of the earth. I have walked at the foot of mountains along long green valleys, I have climbed great ranges and peeped over them, I have lived in barren and in fertile places, and my road-companion has been Nature herself."

I smiled upon my visitor and said, "How like you are to me, my friend! Stay with me and let us talk awhile. Grey days come, and rain, and we shall live in this cave together and converse. In you I see a brother man. In you as in a clear mirror I see the picture of my own soul, a darling shadow. Your songs shall be the words of my happiness, your yearning shall be the expression of my own aching heart. I shall break bread with you and we shall bathe together in the river. I shall sleep with you and wake with you, and be content to see you where'er I turn."

That evening at sunset he crawled with me into the cave. And he slept so sweetly that I held him in my own heart. Next morning at sunrise we clambered out together, and together we gathered sticks, and together bent over the fire and blew into its struggling little flames. Life was rich. We hob-nobbed together. We doubled all our happinesses, and we promised to share all our griefs. Sitting on the rocks—there were many of them about, of all shape and size—we taught one another songs. I wrote songs; he sang them. I told him of places where I had been; he described them to me so that they lived again before me. I told him of beauteous women I had met; he had met them also and revealed to me their loving hearts. He could give the leaping love in my heart a precious name. I verily believe that when the sun was setting golden behind a great cliff, he could bid it stop and shine upon us an hour longer.

Timid and shy at first, he grew more daring afterwards and interpreted my wishes even before I was myself aware of them. He was constantly devising some new happiness. His bird's heart was a fast overflowing fountain.

Then when rainy days came we crouched together in the cave like night-birds sheltered from the day, and we whispered and recounted and planned. I scribbled in my diary in pencil, and he re-wrote my scribbling in bright-coloured chalks, and drew side pictures and wrote poems. Many are the pages we thus wrote together; some he wrote, some I wrote, and there are many from both of us in this volume. When I thought to make a book he laughed and said, "You are making to yourself a graven image." He held it idolatry to imagine that beautiful visions could be represented in words.

"I shall not worship the book," I urged.

"Other people may, or they may revile it", he answered, laughing. "It's the same sin."

"Lest they worship or revile idolatrously, I shall write a notice," said I. "For though I praise Nature ill, and express her ill, she, the wonderful spirit, is beyond all praise or blame." And I wrote these words: "Lest any one should think that in these pages life itself is accounted for, any beauty set down in words, any yearning defined, or sadness utterly plumbed, it is hereby notified that such appreciation is false—that in these pages lies only the symbol of life, the guide-post to the hearts of those who wrote the words. Follow, gentle reader, the directions we have given; tread the roads that we have trod, and see again what we have seen."

To which I added this note: *"The poetry is from my companion's pen, the prose from mine."*

And my companion, not content with that, wrote a postscript: *"There is no prose, and the pen by itself writes nothing at all."*

II. HOW MY COMPANION FOUND HIMSELF IN A COACH

"There is one event in my life that I cannot account for," said my companion, "and it has conditioned all my living, an event psychologically strange. I appear, in a way, to have lost my memory at one era of my existence. I look at the event I am going to relate, and simply stare in perplexed wonder. Somewhere, somewhen, I lost something in my mind! What was that something?

"Most people can tell the story of their life as they themselves remember it. Their memory takes them back to their earliest years, and the memory seems satisfactory to them. But there is a mystery in mine which to my mind remains unexplained. I remember nothing before the age of twenty-one. As far as my memory is concerned I might have been born then. More strange still, I recognise nothing of a past before then, and no one comes out of that past and claims recognition of me.

"This I remember in a dim phantasmal way as the very beginning of things: my getting into a coach in a white mist. Even in that I constantly feel a doubt that my imagination has been playing false with memory. Certainly I do remember finding myself in a coach, but at the startled moment when my conscious life began, it appeared to me that I had never been anywhere in my life but sitting in the coach, A certain intellectual *horror vacuum* may have evoked that mental image of an entering of the coach, but even then I wholly fail to fill in the life and place from which I came. All behind that strange misty entering on the coach-steps is grey, empty mist-land.

"It was a large, smooth-rolling coach, most like a commodious omnibus, and full of a most jovial company. I sat half-way along one of the two lengthy seats, and opposite me was a red-faced man, with large shiny eyes and greasy hair. On one side of me was a jolly country girl of about twenty-five, on the other a thin, dry-looking man. There was an incessant din of conversation and singing; we were leaning towards one another, and saying what jolly fellows we were, we should never part. A bottle was always going round, and every now and then the postilion blew his horn; six horses clattered in front, the dust rolled off behind. I remember myself in a strange state of excitement.

"It was afternoon when I began to think. Actually, at that time I knew I had no memory, but I dared not face the fact. I strove to evade thought by being one of the company. How my cheeks burned as I laughed and talked! I remember pulling a fat man by the sleeve, and whispering in his ear some secret that made us roll back and collapse in laughter. And the coach sped on.

"It seemed an eternal afternoon—chiefly because it filled up all the past for me. I could remember nought before it.

"At last, however, a grand sunset ran scarlet over the whole sky—we still jested, and it was at this time that a little dwarf-like man in a corner appeared fearful to me; there was a fiery reflection of the sunset in his eyes. I saw him once so, I dared not look again. Thoughts were fighting me. My jollity was losing ground. I foresaw that in a short time I should cease to belong to the company, that I should belong utterly to myself, and there would be no escaping from my thoughts. Then at last we passed out of the sunlit country into a place of grey light. It was really natural; the sunset was gone, here was grey twilight. But my disordered mind expected I know not what, either eternal sunset or sudden black night; I cannot say now. I was struck with terror. And standing still with myself, I felt absolutely confounded by the self-question I asked.

" 'Where are we going?'

"Till that moment I had not realised that ignorance of the Past meant ignorance of the Future. I asked where we were going. The laughter and conversation increased. I was answered, but in a jargon I found quite incomprehensible. Another question.

" 'Who under heaven were these people?'

"I stood up and staggered. I must have appeared drunk, for I was greeted with howls and cheers, an inferno of cries and laughter; and the red-faced man stood up also and clung to me, and brought his queer face close up to mine. The girl also clung to me. Then it occurred to me, this was the crisis of a nightmare; in a moment these phantasmal restraints would burst, and I should find myself peacefully—where?

"I remember what seemed a prolonged struggle among laughter and sighs and affectionate clingings, and I got at last out at the door and down the steps. I found myself weakly turning about on my heels on an excessively dusty road. Just ahead of me the coach rolled off into the future stretches of the road, the postilion wound his horn, and the clouds of dust rose up behind the wheels.

"And I was in an open place in the cool of evening. A grey-blue sky above, with the faintest glitter of first stars! I was alone. The past was a mystery; my future unexplored, full of the unimaginable; the ultimate future of course like my past.

"Such was my beginning—the event of my life, in the shadow of which I live and by virtue of which, though I know every road and house of the world, I yet am homeless. No happening in my being, but I must view it in the light of that strange initial mystery. With the problem of that past unsolved, I have never found anything in the ordinary matters of life proposed as all-absorbing occupations. Because of that, I am upon the road. I have made research, and have asked questions of all whom I have met, but I got no answer, and I tired most people with my problem. They say to me lightly, 'Your coach was a dream', and I answer, 'If so, then what before the dream?'"

"We are all of us like you and your coach," I said to my companion. "Some of us know it and some do not, that is all. Some forget the mystery and others remember it."

"*We* remember it," said the wanderer. "Because of it we are irreconcilables, but . . ." he added, looking with a smile at the beautiful world about our cave, "almost reconciled; inconsolable, yet seeing how lovely is this mysterious universe, almost consoled. Most men forget, but many remember; yet whether they remember or no, they are all orphans nevertheless, lost children and homeless ones. We who sing and write and who remember are the voices of humanity. We speak for millions who are voiceless."

III. IRRECONCILABLES

One long sunny morning we talked of the life of the wanderer, and my companion continued his story and recounted how he had found a brotherhood of men like himself.

"When first I found myself thus upon the world, I was full of hope to find an answer to the mystery. But the many fellow-beings I met upon my road were as profitless as my companions in the coach. They could not explain me, they could not explain the world or themselves, and in the midst of teeming knowledges they were obliged to confess one ignorance; among the myriad objects which they could explain they had to acknowledge a whole universe of the inexplicable. I said to them, 'What is all your knowing worth beside the terrible burden of your ignorance, and what are things that you can explain compared with those that are inexplicable?'

"But I found these people proud of their little knowledges, and of the matters they could explain. They were not even startled when I called upon them to remember the great volcano of ignorance, on the slopes of which they were building their little palaces.

"First I despised them, and then I loved them. But I shuddered at the thought that I, an unknown person, unknown to myself and unrecognised by a God, should love people equally unknown—a shadow loved other shadows, and like a shadow I trembled.

"When I learned to love, I felt like a god—just as when the sun learned to warm, he knew that he was a sun. I became like a sun over a little world, and people who did not understand basked in my light and heat.

"But one day love was lost in a cloud, as the sun is lost in a mist which it itself has raised from the earth, and I thought: 'What a fool am I, content to dwell among such people, and be as a king over ***them.*** All that divides me from them is that I know that I know not, and they do not even know that. For they rank their earth knowledge as something more worthy than all their ignorance. I will go forth into the world, and seek for those who are like myself, irreconcilable in front of the inexplicable.'

"I sought them in towns and found them not, for the people, like foolish virgins forgetful of the bridegroom, slumbered and slept. I sought them upon deserts and mountains, and upon the wild plains, but there man was of the earth and beautiful, though not aware of his kingdom beyond the earth. But in the country places I met wise old men who kept candles burning before my shrine, and in the houses of the poor I met the body-wearied, world-defeated, and they, having lost all, found the one hope that I cherished. And in the pages of books, by converse with the dead, I found the great spiritual brotherhood.

"We are many upon the world—we irreconcilables. We cry inconsolably like lost children, 'Oh, ye Gods, have ye forgotten us? Oh, ye Gods, or servants of gods, who abandoned us here, remember us!'

"For perhaps we are kidnapped persons. Perhaps thrones lie vacant on some stars because we are hidden away here upon the earth. I for one have a royal seal on my bosom, a mysterious mark, the sign of a royal house. Ah, my brothers, we are all scions of that house.

"One day I met a man who voluntarily sought death in order to penetrate the mystery of the beyond. But no sign showed itself forth to us, and we know not whether by his desperate deed he won what we have lost, or whether, perchance, he lost all that we can ever win.

"The burden of my ignorance is hard to bear," he cried. The burden of our ignorance is hard to bear. Thus we cry, but there comes no answer, and the eternal silence which enfolds the earth is unbroken. Yet the stars still shine, promising but not fulfilling.

We have become star-gazers, we irreconcilables; expecters of signs and wonders. We live upon every ridge of the world, and have made of every mountain a watch-tower; and from the towers we strain our eyes to see past the stars.

For the stars are perchance but the flowers in a garden, or the lights upon the walls of a garden, and beyond them is the palace of our fathers.

"And since the early days till now," said my companion, "I have wandered about the world, sometimes sojourning a while in a town, but seldom for long. For the town is not a good place."

Then I told him how the town had tempted me, and we compared experiences. We told of the times when we had come nigh forgetting.

"Just think," said I to him, "I should never have found you had I been swallowed up in the town."

"And I should never have lain at your feet in the sun," he replied. "You would never have noticed me in the town."

IV. "HOW THE TOWNSMAN TEMPTED ME"

"Once I was tempted by a townsman," said the wanderer, "but instead of converting me with his town, he was himself converted by the country.

"For many years I wandered by seashores, asking questions of the sea. When I came to the sea it was singing its melancholy song, the song that it has sung from its birth, and it paused neither to hear nor to answer me. Ever rolling, ever breaking, ever weeping, it continued its indifferent labour. I walked along its far-stretching sands, leaving footprints which it immediately effaced. I clambered upon its cliffs and sat looking out to sea for days, my eyes shining like lighthouse fires. But the sea revealed not itself to me. Or perhaps it had no self to reveal. And I could not reveal myself to it; but the sea expressed itself to me as a picture of my mystery.

"I wandered inland to placid lakes, the looking-glasses of the clouds. I threw pebbles into their waters, disturbing their pure reflections, but the disturbances passed away harmlessly into nothingness, and the lakes once more reflected the sky.

"Then I said to my heart, 'We must wander over all the world in search of my homeland, but chance shall not be my guide. I shall loose the reins to thee. Where thou leadest I will follow.'

"I followed my heart through verdant valleys up into a mountain high above a great town. And there for some while I made my abiding place. For I had learned that from a mountain I could see further than from a valley. In the towns my horizons had been all walls, but from this high mountain I looked far over the world.

"One day there came towards my mountain a townsman who tried to lure me to the city below. He was too tired to climb up to me, but from low down he called out, 'You unhappy one, come down out of the height and live with us in the town.

We have learnt the art of curing all sorrow. Let us teach you to forget it, and live among our many little happinesses.'

"And I answered him, 'It is our glory that we shall never forget.' Nevertheless I was tempted and came down.

"The townsman was exceedingly glad, and even before I reached the gates of his city he said to me, 'In after years you will remember me as the man who saved you.'

" 'How?' said I. 'Am I already saved?'

" 'No,' he replied. 'But in the town is your salvation. You will find work to do, and you will not need to return to your mountain to pray. You will understand that work itself is prayer—*laborare est orare.* Your prayer towards the sky was barren and profitless, but prayer towards the earth, ***work,*** will give full satisfaction to your soul.'

"And I mocked him.

" 'What lie is this?' I said. 'How do you dare to confuse labour and prayer? Learn from me, my friend, that work is work, and prayer is prayer. It is written in the old wisdom—"Six parts of thy time shalt thou work for thy bread, and on the seventh thou shalt pray." ***Orare est orare; laborare est laborare.'***

"On the outskirts of the town there were men paving the streets. 'Behold how these men pray!' exclaimed my companion. 'They pave the streets; that is their prayer. They do not gaze at the stars; their eyes are ever on the earth, their home. They have forgotten that there are any stars. They are happy!'

" 'Their souls sleep,' I answered him.

" 'Quite so,' he replied, 'their souls sleep and thus they are happy. They had no use for their souls, therefore we purveyed them sleep, "balm of hurt minds." We gave them narcotics.'

" 'Tell me your narcotics.'

" 'The Gospel of Progress—that is our opium; it gives deep sleep and sweet dreams. It is the most powerful of drugs. When a man takes it once he takes it again, for it tempts him with the prospect of its dreams.'

" 'I shall not taste of it,' said I, 'for I prize Truth above all dreams. What other narcotics have you, sleep-inducing?'

"My companion paused a moment, then replied:

" 'There are two sovereign remedies for the relief of your sorrow, a life of work, or a life of pleasure. But work needs to be done under the influence of the Gospel of Progress. Without a belief in progress, man cannot believe that work is prayer, and that God is a taskmaster. His soul wakes up. He commits suicide or crime. Or he deserts the city, and goes, as you have done, up into the mountains.'

" 'One narcotic helps out the other,' I hazarded.

" 'Quite so. Pleasure is the alternative remedy, a perfectly delightful substitute for your life: wine, the theatre, art, women. But as in taking laudanum, one must graduate the doses—take too much and you are poisoned—'

" 'Wine', I said. 'I have heard of it. It has been praised by the poets, and its service is that it makes one forget! The theatre, its comedies and farces and cunning amusements all designed to help me to forget! Art with its seductions is to obsess the soul with foreign thoughts! Women who languish upon one's eyes and tempt with their beauties, they also would steal away our memories. I will have none of them'.

" 'I spoke of women in general,' said my tempter. 'But think of one woman marvellously wrought for thee, the achiever and finisher of thy being, the answer to all thy questionings, the object of all thy yearnings. In the town thou wilt find the woman for thee, and she will bear thee children.'

" 'You misinterpret my needs, O friend of the town,' I said. 'I do not look to the stars to find a woman. My yearnings are not towards a woman of this earth. Well do I know that you have offered me the most deadly delusion in this woman, **perfectly wrought for my being.** You have taken hold of all my inexpressible yearning and have written over it the word **woman.** And when one of us irreconcilables marries, it often happens that he forgets his loneliness and loses the sense of his mystery. His wife becomes a little house which he lives inside, and his soul is covered up and lost by her. Where he used to see the eternal stars, he sees a woman, and as he understands her, he thinks he understands himself."

" 'But consider,' proceeded my tempter, 'the woman who is exactly the complement of yourself, a woman marvellously and uniquely fashioned to round you off and supply your deficiencies, and use your superfluities.'

" 'If such there be,' I replied, 'I shall not seek her in the town. I know what you mean. I ought to make a home and rear up the second generation. I ought to renounce my own future and dedicate myself to a child so that the mistakes in the old may be set right in the new. I must try to put a child on the road that I missed when I myself was a child, put it in the old coach, perhaps, with a passport in its hand. Even so, that solves no problem, rather multiplies my own problem. What is deathless in man is not answered in that way. What does it profit man that mankind goes on? We cannot tell. But it is clear that we learn nothing new thereby. Rather, as it seems, we forget what we have learned.'

"My friend smiled and said, 'You will think differently later.' Meanwhile he brought me into the heart of his town, a great city of idolaters and opium-eaters. And he took me to the gaming tables of pleasure and the gaming tables of work, and he sought to enchant me with figures and hypnotise me with the gleam of gold.

He showed me how fortunes were made in roulette and in commerce, and tried to bring upon me the gambler's madness. And I smiled and said:

" 'Behold the eyes of yonder gambler; his soul is asphyxied with gold. He pays that homage to the base gleam of a metal that I do to the light of the stars. He is an idolater.'

"In the centre of the city a terrible fear troubled my soul, for it realised that it alone in all this great city of souls preserved its conscience and its wakefulness. By the glare of men's eyes it understood how all were somnambulists. We walked among millions who walked in their sleep. And in their sleep they committed terrible crimes. They looked at me with eyes that saw not; at the bidding of strange dreams they went forward secretly.

"I beheld the thousand mockeries, and chief among them the mockery of our eternal mystery. Instead of the church that is the dome of heaven itself they had built churches of stone. And the people, urged by their dreams, congregated themselves in these churches and were ministered unto by false priests. And dreams of truth conflicted with nightmare enacted themselves. The churches fell out among themselves, and the people fought one another. False priests stood by irresolute, their soft, shapeless lips having been smoothed away by maxims and old words. And they stood in front of idols in a semblance of defence.

"I pushed many priests aside; I thrust my sword through many idols.

" 'Come,' I said, 'your town is terrible. Let me away into my mountain again. You wish me to consider this world worthy of me; you offer me its small things in exchange for my great thing. You have not even small things to offer. Farewell!'

" 'And what is your doctrine?' he said to me at parting. As if we had a doctrine!

" 'For you,' I said, 'the worship of the explained; for us the remembrance of the inexplicable.' "

V. HIS CONVERSION

" 'But your religion?' said the townsman. 'You spoke of your religion. What do you mean by religion?'

" 'Religion is to have charity: never to condemn, never to despair, never to believe that the finite can ever quite cover up the infinite, never to believe that anything is wholly explained, to see the inexplicable in all things, and to remember that words are idols and judgments are blasphemies. For words are the naming of things that are without name, and judgments are the limiting of the wonder of God. And what we call God is the inexplicable, the indefinable, the great Unknown to whom in the midst of the idolatry of Athens an altar was once erected.'

" 'As a child I learnt that God was He who made the world in six days,' said the townsman. 'God was He who delivered unto Moses the ten commandments. Is not this the same which you profess?'

" 'The same,' I answered. 'But you worship Him idolatrously. You limit the wonder of God by words. You limit God's fruitfulness to six days: and you say the world is finished and made. But for us the world is never finished; every spring is a new creation, every day God adds or takes away. And you limit God's laws to ten: you limit the Everlasting Wisdom to ten words. Words are your idols, the bricks out of which your idols and oracles are built. Listen, I will tell you what I have always found in towns. I have found words worshipped as something holy in themselves. Words were used to limit God, debase man. So is it in your town. Once man thought words; now words are beginning to think man. Once man conceived future progress; now your idol Progress is beginning to conceive future man. It is the same as with money; once man made money, but now in your idolatry money makes the man. Once man entered commerce that he might have more life; now he enters life that he may have more commerce. Of women, the very vessels and temples of human life, you have made clerks; of priestesses unto the Living God you have made vestals of the dead gold calf. You have insulted the dignity of man.'

"I waited, but the townsman was silent.

" 'Is that not so?' I urged.

" 'You have your point of view; we have ours. You have your religion and we ours,' said the townsman obstinately. 'And *you* use words, do you not? You have your terminology; you have your idols, just as we have. If not, then how do you use your words?'

"Then I answered him: 'When I found myself upon the world I soon came under the sway of your words. Progress tempted me; commerce promised me happiness. I obeyed commandments and moral precepts, and eagerly swallowed rules of life. I prostrated myself before the great high public idols, I bowed to the little household gods, and cherished dearly your little proverb-idols and maxim-idols. The advice of Polonius to his son and such literature was to me the ancient wisdom. I became an idolater, and my body a temple of idolatry.'

" 'How then did you escape?' asked my companion.

" 'In this wise,' I answered. 'In my temple, as in ancient Athens, in the midst of the idols was an altar to the Unknown God, which altar from the first was present. That altar was to the mystery and beauty of life.

" 'By virtue of this altar I discovered my idolatry, and I recognised the forces of death to which I had bound myself. I broke away and escaped, and in place of all my idols I substituted my aspiring human heart, and it beat like a sacred presence in the clear temple of my being.

" 'Then words I degraded from their fame, and trampling them under my feet, I sang triumphantly to the limitless sky.'

" 'But still you use words,' said the townsman, 'you irreconcilables.'

" 'Yes. When we had degraded their fame and humbled them so that they came to us fawningly, asking to be used, we exalted them to be our servants. Now we are masters over them, and not they over us. They are content to be used, if but for a moment, and then forgotten for ever. We use them to reproduce in other minds the thoughts that are in our own. Woe if they ever get out of hand and become our masters again! They are our exchange metals. Woe if ever again we melt down those metals and recast them as idols!

" 'Come with me into the country,' I urged; and the townsman, as if foreseeing release from the bondage of his soul, allowed my flowing life to float him away from the haunts of his idolatry. Then as we passed from under the canopy of smoke and entered into the bright outside universe, I went on:

" 'Words are become but a small part of our language. We converse in more ways and with more people than of yore. All nature speaks to us; mountain and sea, river and plain, valley and forest; and we reveal our hearts to them, our longing, our hope, our happiness. And yet never entirely reveal. Not with words only do we converse, but with pictures, with music, with scent, with . . . but words cannot name the sacred nameless mediums. And man speaks to man without words; with his eyes, with his hands, with his love. . . .'

"With that we walked some way together silently till at last the townsman put his arm in mine and said: 'In my temple also is an altar with an effaced inscription, methinks to the Ever-Living God. By your words you have revealed it to me. Let me accompany you into the beauty of the world, and interpret thou to me the mystery of its beauty.'

"As if I could interpret!

" 'Behold,' I said, 'forest and mountain, the little copse and the grass under it, and delicate little flowers among the grass. List to the lark's song in the heavens, the wind soughing in the trees, the whispering of the leaves. In the air there is a mysterious incense spread from God's censers, the very language of mystery. Now you see far into the beauty of the world and hear tidings from afar. All the horizons of your senses have been extended. Are you not glad for all these impressions, these pictures and songs and perfumes? Every impression is a shrine, where you may kneel to God.'

" 'It is a beautiful world,' said he.

" 'It is beautiful in all its parts and beautiful every moment,' I replied. 'My soul constantly says *"Yes"* to it. Its beauty is the reminder of our immortal essence. The town is dangerous in that it has little beauty. It causes us to forget. It is exploring the illusion of trade, and its whole song is of trade. If you understand this, you have a criterion for Life—

" ' *The sacred is that which reminds us; the secular is that which bids us forget.*

" 'When you have impressions of sight, noise, and smell, and these impressions have no shrine where one may kneel to God, it is a sure sign that you have forgotten Him, that you are dwelling in the courts of idols.'

" 'But it is painful to remember,' said my companion, 'and even now I have great pain. It is hard to leave the old, and painful to receive the new. My heart begins to ache for loneliness, and I long for the gaiety of the town and its diversions. I should like once more to drown my remembrances.'

"I bade him have courage, for he was in the pains of birth. The old never lets out the new without pain and struggle, but when the new is born it is infinitely worthy. And my new friend was comforted. We spent many days upon the road, looking at beauty, conversing with one another, worshipping and marvelling. Along the country paths flowers looked up, and beautiful suns looked out of strange skies. Often it seemed we had been together upon the same road a thousand years before.

Was it a remembrance of the time before my entering into the coach? The flowers by the roadside tried to whisper a word of the answer to my question. It seemed that we were surrounded by mysteries just about to reveal themselves. Or, anon, it seemed as if we had missed our chance, as if an unseen procession had just filed by and we had not distinguished it.

"My friend was leaving behind all his idols. We sat upon a ridge together, and looked back upon the valley and the city which we had left. There was what my soul abhorred, and what I feared his soul might be too weak to face—the kaleidoscope of mean colours turning in the city, tickling our senses, striving to bind our souls and to mesmerise. Some colours would have drawn our tears, some would have persuaded smiles over our lips. Combinations of colours, groupings, subtle movements and shapings sought to interest and absorb our intellects.

" 'Behold,' said I. 'In the city which calls itself the world, the townsmen are casting up dice! Is it possible we shall be stricken with woe, or immensely uplifted in joy because of the falling of a die? Oh world too sordid to be opposed to us! Oh world too poor to be used by us! Is not the world's place under our feet, for it is of earth and we of spirit?'

"But my friend was not with me. He wavered as if intoxicated, and wished to return to the city. 'Oh glorious world,' said he, and sighed himself towards the gates we had left.

"Then seeing the brightness of my face, which just then reflected a great brightness in the sky, and remembering that his pain was only a bridge into the new, he gained possession of himself and turned his eyes away from the town.

" 'More than my old self and its weak flesh do I value the new young life that is to be,' said he. 'Though I am a man and a creature of pleasure, I am become as a woman that bears children. For the time is coming when I shall give birth to one younger than myself, later than myself. . . .'

" 'Your old self will reappear more beautiful, new-souled, transfigured,' I replied.

"Then my companion looked at me with eyes that were full both of yearning and of pain, and he said, 'Though I would fain stay with you, yet must I go apart. For I have one battle yet to fight, and that I can only fight alone. Farewell, dear friend, husband of the woman that is in me!'

"Then said I farewell and we embraced and parted, for I saw that it was meet for him to commune alone with God and gain strength to win his victory.

"The town lay in the west; he went into the north and I into the east. Once more I was alone."

"Come, let us devise new means of happiness," said my companion. "Let us wander up-stream to the silent cradle of the river. For all day long I hear the river calling my name."

And we journeyed a three days' tramp into the mountains, following the silver river upward and upward to the pure fountain of its birth. And on the way, moved by the glow of intercourse, I told my companion the story of Zenobia, and also that of the old pilgrim whom I met at New Athos. It was strange to us that the peasants in the country should live and die so much more worthily than the educated folk who live in the towns. God made the country, man made the town, and the devil made the country town, was not for us an idle platitude but a burning fact, though we agreed that man was often a much more evil creator than the devil, and that the great capitals of Europe and America were the worst places for Man's heavenly spirit that Time had ever known.

Imagine our three days' journeying, the joy of the lonely one who has found a companion, the sharing of happiness that is doubling it; the beauty to live in, the little daintinesses and prettinesses of Nature to point out; the morning, sun-decked and dewy, the wide happiness of noon, the shadows of the great rocks where we rested, and the flash of the green and silver river tumbling outside in the sunshine; quiescent evening and the old age of the day, sunset and the remembrance of the day's glory, the pathos of looking back to the golden morning.

The first night we made our bed where the plover has her nest, in a grassy hollow on the shelf of a mountain.

"The day is done," said my companion. "A little space of time has died. Now see the vision of the Eternal, which comes after death;" and he pointed to the night sky, in which one by one little lamps were lighting.

The bright world passed away, faded away in my eyes and became at last a dark night sky in which shone countless stars. During the day, my soul expressed itself to itself in the beauty which is for an hour, but at night it re-expressed itself in terms of the Infinite. I looked to my companion, and his eyes and lips shone in the darkness so that he seemed dressed in cloth cut from the night sky itself, and interwoven with stars. We lay together and looked up into the far high sky, we breathed lightly: it seemed we exhaled the scent of flowers that we had inbreathed in the morning—we slept.

And then the morning! The quiet, quiet hours, the flitting of moths in the dawn twilight, the mysterious business of mice among the stones about us, the cold fleeting air just before sunrise, full of ghosts, our own awakening and the majestic sunrise, the exaggeration of all shapes, the birth of shadows, the beaming heralds, glorious rose-red summits and effulgent silvered crags, ten thousand trumpets raised to the zenith, and ten thousand promises outspoken!

We arose, my companion and I—he only seemed to come to life when the first beam touched me. I greeted the sun with my voice, and turning round, there at my feet was my friend, familiar, dear, so ready for living that one would have said the sun himself was his father.

"I was dead," said he, "and behold I am alive again. The world passed away, and behold, at the voice of a trumpet, it hath come back. Beauty faded yestreen from colour into darkness, from life to death, and to-day it hath out-blossomed once again; the Sun was its father, dear gentle Night its mother. . . ."

And running with me, he clambered upon a rock and outstretched his arms to the sun as if he were a woman looking to a strong man.

"Greater is the glory of sunrise than the glory of sunset, for the sunrise promises what shall be, whereas the sunset only tells the glory of the past. The sunrise promises beautiful days, the sunset looks back upon beauty as if there were nothing in the future to compare with what has just departed."

Thus sang my friend, and we scampered along to the newly wakened river. Cold and fresh was the water, as if it also had slept in the night. It was full of the night, but the morning which was in us strove with it, and at a stroke conquered it. The sun laughed to see us playing in the water, and we greeted him with handfuls of sparkles. The river was lusty and strong; it wrestled with us, grasped, pushed, pulled, buffeted, threw stones, charged forward in waves, laboriously rolled boulders against us. . . .

We made our morning fire; its blue smoke rose slowly and crookedly, and the brittle wood burning crackled like little dogs barking; the kettle hissed on the hot, black stones where we had balanced it over the fire, it puffed, it growled, blew out its steam and boiled, boiled over; tea, bread and cheese, bright yellow plums from a tree hard by, and then away once more we sped on our journey, not walking, but running, scarcely running but flying, leaping, clambering . . . and my companion performed the most astonishing feats, for he was ever more lively than I was.

The sun strengthened. First it had empowered us to go forward, but after some hours it bid us rest. Seven o'clock ran to eight, eight to nine; nine to ten was hot, ten was scorching, and by eleven we were conquered. We rested and let the glorious husband of the earth look down upon us, and into us.

"How pathetic it is that men are even now at this moment sweating, and grinding, and cursing in a town," said my companion to me. He was lying outstretched before me on a slope of the sheep-cropped downs. "They altogether miss life, life, the inestimable boon. And they get nothing in return. Even what they hope to gain is but dust and ashes. They waited perhaps a whole eternity to be born, and when they die it may be that for a whole eternity they must wait again. God allotted them each year eighty days of summer and eighty summers in their lives, and they are content to sell them for a small price, content to earn wages. . . . And their share in all this beauty, they hardly know of it, their share in the sun.

"Have you not realised that we have more than our share of the sun? The sun is fuller and more glorious than we could have expected. That is because millions of people have lived without taking their share. We feel in ourselves all *their* need of it, all their want of it. That is why we are ready to take to ourselves such immense quantities of it. We can rob no one, but, on the contrary, we can save a little to give to those who have none—when we meet them. You must pull down the very sun from heaven and put it in your writings. You must give samples of the sun to all those who live in towns. Perhaps some of those attracted by the samples will give up the smoke and grind of cities and live in this superfluity of sunshine."

Then I said to my joyous comrade: "Many live their lives of toil and gloom and ugliness in the belief that in another life after this they will be rewarded. They think that God wills them to live this life of work."

"Then perhaps in the next life they will again live in toil and gloom, postponing their happiness once more," said my companion. "Or on the Day of Judgment they will line up before God and say with a melancholy countenance, 'Oh Lord we want our wages for having lived!' . . . An insult to God and to our glorious life, but how terrible, how unutterably sad! And the reply of the angel sadder still, 'Did you not know that life itself was a reward, a glory?' "

V

THE UNCONQUERABLE HOPE

ONCE, long ago, when an earthquake rent the hills, and mountains became valleys, and the earth itself opened and divided, letting in the sea, a new island was formed far away upon an unvisited ocean. Out of an inland province of a vast continent this island was made, all the land upon it having been submerged, and all the peoples that dwelt to north and to south, to east and to west, having been drowned.

There survived upon the island a few men and women who remained undisputed masters of the land, and they lived there and bred there. No one visited them, for the island was remote, unknown; and they visited no one, for they had never seen the sea before, they had not even known of its existence, and they did not know how to fashion a boat.

The island became fertile, and men and women married, and bore sons and daughters. The people in the island multiplied and grew rich. But all the while they lived without the invention of the boat, and they thought their island was the whole world, not knowing of the other lands that lay beyond the sea.

The original people died in their time, and their sons and daughters and grandsons and granddaughters, and the newer, later, survived and gave birth to newer and later still. And the story of the origin of the island was handed down from generation to generation.

The story was a matter of fact. It became history, it became legend and tradition, it became a myth, it became almost the foundation of religion. For a thousand years a lost family of mankind dwelt on that island on the unvisited sea, and none of their kindred ever came out of its barren sea-horizons to claim them.

And then, lest these children of men should utterly forget, a child was born who should understand. As happens once in many centuries, a wise man arose, and he interpreted the legends and traditions, and refreshed in the memory of this people the significance of their origin.

He taught them the mystery of the sea, and of the beyond, that hitherto unimaginable beyond, so that men yearned to cross the ocean.

Then the ignorant rose up and slew that man, thinking him an evil one, luring men to their death. And those who had understood him sorrowed greatly. His life had been pure, white, without reproach, and the light that shone in his eyes was the same that burned in the stars.

But though the ignorant could destroy his body, they could not destroy the fair life that he had lived, that wonderful example of how men may stand in the presence of the eternal mysteries.

There arose followers who dedicated themselves to the truth he had revealed, that truth boundless and infinite as the sea itself. And they lit a fire like the sacred fire in the temples of the fire-worshippers, and that fire should never be extinguished until some sign rose out of the horizon, illumining and dissolving the mystery.

"Who knows," they say, "but that we are the descendants of kings? There is that in us that is foreign to this land, something not indigenous to this soil, of which this island is not worthy. It cometh from afar and had elsewhere its begetting. In us are latent unnamed powers, senses that in this island cannot be used. Our eyes are unnecessarily bright, our hearts superfluously strong. This Earth cannot satisfy us, it cannot afford scope enough, we cannot try ourselves upon it. This is the hope that we keep holy, that out of the heavens or across the sea our kindred, our masters, or our gods will claim us and take us to a new land where our hearts' meaning may completely show itself outwardly to the sky; where our latent senses will find the things that can be sensed, and our faculties that which can be made, where our hearts and wills may be satisfied, and we may find wings with which to soar over all seas."

Behold these dedicates, with their torch of remembrance kindled in the night of ignorance, these living eternally in the presence of the mystery! They pine upon shores, looking over the unbridgeable abyss, yearning their souls towards that ultimate horizon, with limbs vainly strong, eyes vainly keen, hearts ready for an adventure they may not undertake. At their feet wails the sea with never-ending sadness. In their minds are haunting tunes, the echoes of the wailing of the waves. They cry, and no one hears; they sing, and no one responds; they are like those who have loved once and lost, and who may never be comforted.

These nurse in their hearts the unconquerable hope.

So is it with us upon the world, we irreconcilable ones; we stand upon many shores and strain our eyes to see into the unknown. We are upon a deserted island and have no boats to take us from star to star, not only upon a deserted island but upon a deserted universe, for even the stars are familiar; they are worlds not unlike our own. The whole universe is our world and it is all explained by the scientists, or is explicable. But beyond the universe, no scientist, not any of us, knows anything. On all shores of the universe washes the ocean of ignorance, the ocean of the inexplicable. We stand upon the confines of an explored world and gaze at many blank horizons. We yearn towards our natural home, the kingdom in which our spirits were begotten. We have rifled the world, and tumbled it upside-down, and run our fingers through all its treasures, yet have not come upon the charter of our birth. We explored Beauty till we came to the shore of a great sea; we explored music, and came upon the outward shore of harmony and earthly truth, and found its limits.

Some spoke of our limitations, but it is our glory that our hearts know no limitations except those which are the defects of the world. The world is full of limitations, but our hearts scorn them, being full of boundless power.

Some day for us shall come into that blank sky-horizon which is called the zenith, a stranger, a man or a god, perhaps not like ourselves, yet having affinities with ourselves, and correlating ourselves to some family of men or gods of which we are all lost children. We shall then know our universal function and find our universal orbit.

As yet the True Sun stands in the antipodes, the great light is not vouchsafed. In the night of ignorance our little sun is shining and stars gleam upon our sky-horizons. But when the True Sun shines their brightness will be obscured, and we shall know a new day and a new night, a new heaven and a new earth.

It is written, "When He appears we shall be like Him."

VI

THE PILGRIMAGE TO JERUSALEM

I

ONCE, possibly, upon the world, man did not know of God; he had not looked to the blank horizon and spoken to the Someone beyond. He had all the need to speak, all the oppression in his soul, all the sorrow and longing pent up in him and the tears unshed, but knew no means of relief, did not even conceive of any one beyond himself. He had no great Father, as we have. A strange, unhappy life he lived upon the world, uncomforted, unfriended. He looked at the stars and comprehended them not; and at the graves, and they said nought. He walked alone under heaven's wide hollowness.

We of later days have God as a heritage, or if we did find Him of ourselves, the road was made easy for us. But some one far away back in human life found God first, and said to Him the first prayer; some hard, untutored savage found out the gentlest and loveliest fact in our religion. A savage came upon the pearl and understood it and fell down in joy. A man one day named God and emptied his heart to Him in prayer. And he told the discovery to his brothers, and men all began to pray. The world lost half its heaviness at once. Men learned that their prayers were nearly all the same, that God heard the same story from thousands and hundreds of thousands of hearts. Thus men came nearer to one another, and knew themselves one in the presence of God, and they prayed together and formed churches. Man, the homeless one, had advanced a step towards his home, for he began to live partly in the beyond.

I am reminded of this by the joy which accompanies the personal discovery of some new rite which brings us into relation with the unseen.

Following that hypothetical first man, how many real first men there have been, each discovering new things about God and the beyond, giving mankind new letters in the Sanscrit, and each discovery accompanied by joy and relief.

The conception of life as part of a journey to the heavenly city was, I think, one of these discoveries; and its rite was the church procession to the altar. In symbolic act man learned to make the journey beyond the blank horizon. He enlarged the church procession to the pilgrimage to Jerusalem, and he enlarged the pilgrimage to Jerusalem to the pilgrimage of life itself. In the understanding of life as a pilgrimage, the wanderer and seeker has the world for his church.

We are all on the road to the City of Jerusalem. Those who are consciously on the road may call themselves pilgrims; they have a life of glory in the heart as well as of toiling by the way. They are in a certain definite perspective, and they see all things that happen to them in the light of the pilgrimage. I for my part, directly I definitely set out for Jerusalem, on the very first day, at the sight of the first stranger who crossed my path, exclaimed to myself, "I meet him on the way to Jerusalem; that makes a difference, does it not?"

But not only does the goal of the pilgrimage lend a new significance to the present and the future; it also lights up the past. It makes every idlest step of worth. It makes us so understanding of the past that we would not alter one jot or tittle in it. Our whole life is transfigured. Every deed of our hands, every thought of our minds and word of our lips, every deed of others or of Nature seen, every word of man or sound of Nature heard, is made into one glowing garment—the story of our life-pilgrimage *via* the present moment to the Heavenly City.

I started on my pilgrimage long ago, so long ago I can hardly tell when. As Jeremy the pilgrim said of Mikhail: "He wished to go when he was a little boy; that means, he began to go then, for whenever you begin to wish you begin the pilgrimage. After that, no matter where you are, you are sure to be on the way." It is a stage in the awakening of consciousness, that wishing to go; the next stage is intending to go, and the next, deciding to go and setting out—but independently of these wishes and intentions and decisions, we were really on the road, and going all the while. By our true wishes we divine our destiny.

Yes, even long ago I wished, and to-day I am still on the way, though I have actually pilgrimaged to Jerusalem in Palestine. My pilgrimage was a pilgrimage within a pilgrimage. It was the drawing of a picture on earth of a journey in heaven. As a day is to a year, and as a year to man's life, so is man's life to that which we do not know, the course of our life beyond Time's blank horizon. If I have often stopped to tell of a little day, or a little hour in the day, it is because I sought there a picture of Eternity, of the whole significance of the pilgrimage.

I suppose I did not know that when I first left England to go to Russia I was turning my face toward Jerusalem. Yet it was so. For I should never have gone direct from London to the Holy Land. If I had attempted such a journey I should probably have failed to reach the great Shrine, for it is only a certain sort of people travelling in a certain sort of way who find admittance easily. By the Russian peasant I was enabled to go. It is strange to think that even when I was journeying northward to Archangel I was winding my way Jerusalem-ward in the sacred labyrinth. And I could not have gone straight southward with the pilgrims without wandering in contrary directions first of all, for it was necessary to come into sympathy and union with the peasant soul. There is a peasant deep down in my soul, or a peasant soul deep down in me, as well as an exterior, sensitive, cultured soul. I had to discover that peasant, to realise myself as one of the poor in spirit to whom is the kingdom.

Christ preached His gospel to the peasant. His is a peasant's gospel, it seems to me, such a gospel as the peasants of Russia would take to themselves to-day if Jesus came preaching to them in the way He did to the common ***people*** of the Jews. The cultured would disdain it, until a new St. Paul interpreted it for them in terms that they could understand, so giving it a "vogue." Both the peasants and the cultured would be Christians, but with this difference, that in one case the seed would be growing on the surface, and in the other from the depths. The peasant, of course, has no ***surface;*** he is the good black earth all ready for the seed.

There is a way for the cultured: it is to discover the peasant down beneath their culture, the original elemental soil down under the artificial surface, and to allow the sweetness and richness of that soil to give expression on that surface. True culture is thus achieved; that which is not only on the surface but of the depths.

Thereby might every one discover not only the peasant but the pilgrim soul within; each man living on the world might realise himself as on the way to Jerusalem. Such realisation would be the redemption of the present culture of the West. For workers of every kind—not only artists, musicians, novelists, but the handicraftsmen, the shapers of useful things, of churches and houses and laws, even the labourers in the road and the garden—would be living in the strength of a promise and the light of a vision.

The pilgrimage was a carrying of the cross, but it was also a happy wayfaring. It was a hard journey but not comfortless. Many of the pilgrims walked thousands of miles in Russia before finally embarking on the pilgrim boat. They walked solitarily, not in great bands, and they were poor. From village to village, from the Far North, Central Russia and the East, they tramped their way to Odessa and Batoum, and they depended all the way on other men's hospitality. As Jeremy said, "They had no money: instead of which they found other men's charity." They lived night by night in hundreds of peasant homes, and prayed day by day in hundreds of little churches. Not only did they find their daily bread "for the love of God," but in many cases they were furnished even to Jerusalem itself with passage money for the boat journey, and bread to keep the body alive.

Such pilgrims often were illiterate, and it was astonishing how they remembered all the folk they had to pray for at Jerusalem; for every poor peasant who could not leave his native village, but gave threepence or four-pence to the wanderer, asked to be remembered in the land "where God walked." Perhaps there were aids to remembrance. Many people in the villages, wanting to be sure that their prayers and wants would be remembered, wrote their names on slips of paper and thrust them into the pilgrim's hand. Thus in the hostelry at Jerusalem an old wanderer came to me one morning with a sheaf of dirty papers on which were written names, and I read them out for him aloud, thus:—

Maria for health.
Katerina for health.
Rheumatic Gregory for health.
Ivan for the peace of soul of his mother.
For the peace of soul of Prascovia.

And so on; and I sorted them into separate bundles—those who wished prayers for health, and those who wanted peace of soul to the dead.

I, for my part, have walked many a thousand versts from village to village, and have been glad to live the peasant-pilgrim's life. Tramping was hard for me also, as also far from comfortless. I saw sights which amply repaid me, if I wanted repayment, for every verst I tramped. Often, and shamefully, have I looked back and sighed for the town that I had left—its friends, its comforts and its pleasures; but I also found other men's hospitality and the warmth of the stranger's love. Very sweet it was to sit in the strange man's home, to play with his children on the floor, to eat and drink with him, to be blessed by him and by his wife, and sleep at last under the cottage ikons. And though peasants knew the way was hard, "How fortunate you are!" they said. I was more fortunate than they knew, for, being the voice of those who were without voice, I had a life by the way in communion with every common sight and sound. I lived in communion with sunny and rainy days, with the form of mountain and valley, with the cornfield and the forest and the meadow. Not only was man hospitable to the tramp, but Nature also. The stars spoke of my pilgrimage, the sea murmured to me; wild fruit was my food. I slept with the bare world as my house, the sky as my roof, and God as host.

I saw strange happenings in obscure little villages. Wherever I went I saw little pictures, and not only great pageants; I knelt in little wooden churches as well as in the great cathedrals. And I brought all that I met and all that I had experienced to Jerusalem, so that when the chorus of thanksgiving went up in the monastery on the day when we arrived, all my world was singing in it.

Sometimes I met pilgrims, especially at monasteries, and sometimes sojourned with one along the road, but it was not until we reached the pilgrim-boat that we found ourselves many and together. For the greater part of the pilgrim life is necessarily in solitude. A great number of pilgrims starting together and marching along the road is almost unthinkable. The true desire to start takes one by oneself. The pilgrim life is born like a river, far away apart, up in the mountains. It is only when it is reaching its goal that it joins itself to others. When we reached the port of embarkation we were a great band of pilgrims, but the paths by which we had come together were many and diverse, ramifying all over Russia.

We thought, but for the haunting fear of storms, that when we reached the boat the arduous part of our journey would have been accomplished. We should cease our plodding over earth, and should rest on the sea in the sun. We would sing hymns together. Hymns are, of course, principally designed for pilgrims, for man as a pilgrim, who needs to console himself with music on the road. We would talk among ourselves of our life on the way; the days would go past in pleasant converse and the nights in happy slumber. But that was a mistake. The sea journey was worse than any of our tramping; it was the very crown of our suffering.

There were 560 of us packed into the holds of that hulk, the **Lazarus,** on which we sailed, and there were besides, many Turks, Arabs, and Syrians; of cattle, two score cows and a show bull with two mouths; of beasts, a cage of apes; and, as if to complete pandemonium in storm, there lay bound in his bed on the open deck a raving madman. We were a fortnight on the sea, wandering irrelevantly from port to port of the Levant, discharging a cargo of sugar; and all the while the poor beggar-pilgrims lived on the crusts of which they had sackfuls collected in Russia, crusts of black bread all gone green with mould. I looked at the piles of them heaped on the deck to air in pleasant weather, and was amazed that men could live simply on decay. We had two storms, in one of which our masts were broken down and we were told we should go to the bottom. The peasants rolled over one another in the hold like corpses, and clutched at one another like madmen. In despair some offered all their money, all that they had, to a priest as a votive offering to St. Nicholas, that the storm might abate. The state of the ship I should not dare to depict—the filth, the stench, the vermin. For nearly a thousand passengers there were three lavatories without bolts! Fitly was the boat named **Lazarus**—Lazarus all sores. What the poor simple peasant men and women suffered none can tell. They had, not the thought to take care of themselves as I had, and indeed they would have scorned to save themselves. "It is necessary to suffer," they said.

It was a hard and terrible way, and yet on the last day of the voyage, in the sight of the Holy Land, our hearts all leapt within us with grateful joy. We felt it was worth it, every whit. When I think of this journey as of that of Christian in the **Pilgrim's Progress,** I call this ship and the journey on it the Valley of the Shadow of Death, full of foul pits and hobgoblins; something which must be passed through if Jerusalem is to be attained; the dread gulf which lies between earthly and heavenly life. It was necessary to pass through it, and what was on the other side was infinitely worth the struggle. There is a story in Dostoievsky of a Russian free-thinker whose penance beyond this world was to walk a quadrillion versts. When he finished this walk and saw the Heavenly City at the end of it he fell down and cried out, "It is worth it, every inch; not only would I walk a quadrillion of versts, but a quadrillion of quadrillions raised to the quadrillionth power."

II

At last we arrived at Jerusalem. The onlookers saw a long, jaded-looking flock of poor people toiling up the hilly road from Jaffa, wearing Russian winter garb under the straight-beating sun of the desert, dusty, road-worn, and beaten. We went along the middle of the roadway like a procession, observed of all observers; in one sense scarcely worth looking at, yet in another the most significant spectacle of the day or of the time. We were—religious Europe just arrived at the Heavenly City.

Certainly it would have been difficult to know the happiness and exaltation of our hearts; perhaps to do that it would have been necessary to step into line and follow us to the Cathedral and the Sepulchre; perhaps even necessary to anticipate our coming, and join us long before, on the way in Russia.

But we went forward unconscious of our own significance, indifferent to the gaze of the curious. There was one thought in our minds: that we had actually attained unto Jerusalem and were walking the last few miles to the Holy of Holies.

We passed in through the gate of the Russian settlement, and in a moment were at the monastery doors. How gladly we threw off our packs on the green grass sward and hurried into church to the Thanksgiving Service, buying sheaves of little candles at the door and pressing in to light them before the sacred ikons. When the priest was given the great Bible to read, it lay on the bare heads of pilgrims; so close did the eager ones press together to share in the bearing that the Holy Book needed no other support. We sang the **Mnogia Lieta** with a deep harmonious chorus; we prostrated ourselves and prayed and crossed. I stood in the midst and sang or knelt with the rest, timid as a novice, made gentle by the time, and I learned to cross myself in a new way. One by one the peasants advanced and kissed the gold cross in the hands of the priest, and among them I went up and was blessed as they were. And we were all in rapture. Standing at the threshold afterwards, smiling peasants with wet shining eyes confessed to one another their unworthiness and their happiness; and a girl all in laughing tears fell down at our feet, kissing our dusty boots, and asking our forgiveness that she had been permitted to see Jerusalem.

We were taken to the refectory and seated at many tables to a peasant dinner: cabbage soup and porridge, bread and **kvass,** just as they are served in Russia itself. We passed to the hostelry and were given, at the rate of three farthings a day, beds and benches that we might occupy as long as we wished to stay in Jerusalem. The first night we were all to get as rested as possible, the next we were to spend in the Sepulchre itself. I slept in a room with four hundred peasants, on a wooden shelf covered with old pallets of straw. The shelves were hard and dirty; there was no relaxation of our involuntary asceticism, but we slept well. There was music in our ears. We had attained to Jerusalem, and our dreams were with the angels. Jerusalem the earthly had not forced itself upon our minds; we held the symbolism of the journey lightly, and the mind read a mystery in delicate emotions. The time was to come when some of us would be discontented with Jerusalem, as some of the disciples who fell away were discontented with the poor and humble Jesus; but as yet even to these all the material outward appearance of Jerusalem was a rumour. We knew not what we should see when we stepped out on the morrow; perhaps pearly gates, streets of gold, angels with harps. Jerusalem the earthly was unproved. We had as yet only toiled up the steep Jaffa way, and the road to heaven itself might be not unlike that road. To-morrow . . . who could say what to - morrow would unfold? For those of us who could see with the eyes of the heart there could be no disappointment. But for all, this night of golden dreams was a respite, and Jerusalem the symbol and Jerusalem the symbolised were one. Happy, happy pilgrims!

Next day we went to the strange and ugly church erected over the Sepulchre of Jesus, the "Church of the Life-giving Grave"; and we kissed the stone of anointing— the stone on which the body of Jesus lay whilst it was being wrapped in fair linen and anointed with oil. We knelt before the ark-like inner temple which is built over **the hollow in the rock.** We were received into that temple, and one by one crept along the passage-way to the Holy of Holies, the inmost shrine of Christendom. Only music could tell what the peasant realised in that chamber as he knelt where the sacred Body lay, and kissed the hollow in the stone.

Then we spent a whole night in the Sepulchre and entered into the mystery of death—saw our own death as in a picture before us, our abiding in the grave until the resurrection. In the great dark church the solemn service went forward. On the throne of the altar at Golgotha near by, the candles gleamed. Night grew quiet all around, and the Syrian stars looked over us, so that centuries and ages passed away.

III

We went through the life of Jesus in symbolical procession, journeyed to Bethlehem and kissed the manger where the baby Jesus was laid, that first cradle as opposed to the second, the hollow in the rock. We came as the Kings, saw the shepherds and their flocks, saw the star stop over the house of Mary, and went in to do homage, bringing thither the gifts of our hearts—gold, frankincense, and myrrh.

We tramped to the river Jordan, and all in our death shrouds at Bethabara, waded into the stream and were baptized. In symbolic act the priest baptizing us was veritably John, but in second symbolism it was Jesus. As we stepped down into the water it was John, but when we stepped up again it was Jesus receiving us into light. We made a picture of the past, but we had also in our hearts a presentment of the far future. As we stood there on the banks all in our white robes it seemed like a rehearsal of the final resurrection morning. These shrouds in which the pilgrims are baptized they preserve to their death day, in order that they may be buried in them. They believe that on the Last Day not only will their bodies of this day be raised up, but the Jordan washed garments will be restored as well.

We followed the course of the river down to the Dead Sea, the lowest place on earth, and thence walked across the wilderness to the Mountain of Temptation, where in innumerable caves had lived thousands of hermits and saints. In a great caravan we journeyed to the Lake of Galilee, where the Twelve were called. We camped upon the mountain where the five thousand had been fed, and scattered bread there. We dwelt in the little town of Nazareth and saw the well where Mary had drawn water. We heard of all the dear-nesses which the priests and monks had imagined as likely in the boyhood of Jesus. We stood and wondered at the place where Mary and Joseph are supposed to have stopped and missed their twelve-year-old son who had gone to the Temple to teach. We stood where Jesus had conversed with the woman of Samaria. We visited the cottage where the water was changed into wine. At Bethany we prayed at Lazarus' grave.

We lived with the life of Jesus as the story has been told. It was a second pilgrimage, an underlining of the essentials of the first. We finished the first pilgrimage at the Church of the Tomb on the day after our arrival in Jerusalem; we should finish the second on the last day of Holy Week, at the triumphant Easter morning.

On the Friday before Palm Sunday we went out to Bethany and slept in the monastery which is built "where Martha served." Next day we returned to Jerusalem with olive branches, palms and wild flowers, scattering blossoms as we walked. On Saturday evening and in the morning of Palm Sunday we filled the churches with our branches. Two aged pilgrims who had died were buried on Palm Sunday. They lay in open coffins in church dressed in the shrouds they had worn at Jordan, covered with olive branches and little blue wild flowers (Jacob's ladder), which the pilgrims had picked for them at Bethany. On their faces was perfect peace. The pilgrims thought them happy to die in the Holy Land and be buried there.

The crown of the pilgrimage was Holy Week. By Palm Sunday all the pilgrims were back in Jerusalem from their little pilgrimages to Nazareth, Jericho, and Jordan. The hostelries were crowded. Fully five hundred men and women slept in the hall in which I was accommodated. All night long the sound of prayer and hymn never died away. At dawn each day a beggar pilgrim sanctified our benches with incense which he burned in an old tin can. By day we visited the shrines of Jerusalem, the Virgin's tomb, the Mount of Olives, the Prætorium, Pilate's house, the dungeon where Jesus was put in the stocks. We saw the washing of the feet on Holy Thursday; we walked down the steep and narrow way where Christ carried the cross and stumbled, kissed the place where Saint Veronica held out the cloth which took the miraculous likeness. We examined our souls before Good Friday; we went to the special yearly Holy Communion now invested with a strange and awful solemnity. There was the prostration before the Cross at Golgotha on Good Friday, the receiving of the Sacred Fire, symbol of the Resurrection, on Holy Saturday, and then the night of the year and the Great Morning. It seemed when we all kissed one another on Easter Morning that we had outlived everything—our own life, our own death; we were in heaven. In symbolic act we had attained unto bliss. The procession had marched round the church to the supreme emotional moment. We had all stood on the highest holy place on earth and looked out for a moment upon Paradise. We had caught the gleam of the Sun of another universe.

What happens in the pilgrim's soul on Easter Night is something which you and I and all of us know; if not in our own minds and in the domain of letters and words, at least in the heart where music speaks. To those who have not themselves attained unto Jerusalem and the "highest of all earthly" it is a promise, and to those who have been it is a memory and a possession. The Greek monks say that at the sepulchre a fire bursts out of its own account each Easter Eve, and there is at least a truth of symbolism in their miracle. An old bishop and saint was once asked to give sight to a blind woman. He had performed no miracles in his life, yet he promised to pray for her. And whilst he knelt in church praying, the candles which were unlit burst of themselves into flame. The woman at that moment also received her sight and went home praising God. It is something like that which happens when the pilgrim kneels on Easter Night. Candles unlit in the temple of his soul burst into flame, and by their light new pictures are seen. The part of him that was blind and craved sight gains open eyes at that moment, and that which seemed impossible is accomplished.

IV

And I, to use the metaphor of the unvisited island, had in a dream crossed the ocean, had become, through the fulfilling of a rite, more bound to the life which is beyond. Henceforth I have a more credible promise and a more substantial hope.

But what then? The journey is ended, the gleam of the vision fades, and we all return to the life we came from. We descend from what the pilgrims call the highest holy place on earth and get back to the ordinary level of life. How can we go back and live the dull round again? Shall we not be as Lazarus is depicted in Browning's story of him, spoiled for earth, having seen heaven? The Russian at home calls the returned pilgrim *polu-svatoe,* a half-saint: does that perhaps mean that life is spoilt for him?

Some hundreds of aged pilgrims die every year in Lent; they fall dead on the long tramps in Galilee on the way to Nazareth. Many pass peacefully away in Jerusalem itself without even seeing Easter there. They are accounted happy. To be buried at Jerusalem is considered an especially sweet thing, and it is indeed very good for these aged ones that the symbol and that which it symbolised should coincide, and that for them the journey to Jerusalem the earthly should be so obviously and materially a big step towards Jerusalem the golden. It would have been sad in a way for such old folk to return once more across the ocean to the old, somewhat irrelevant life of Mother Russia. But what of the young who must of necessity go back?

Once Easter was over it was marvellous how eager we were to get on the first boat and go home again. What were we going to do when we got there, seeing that we had been to Jerusalem?

We carry our vision back into daily life, or rather, we carry the memory of it in our hearts until a day of fulfilment. All true visions are promises, and that which we had was but a glimpse of a Jerusalem we shall one day live in altogether.

The peasants took many pictures of the sacred places of Jerusalem, and Jerusalem ikons, back with them to their little houses in Russia, there to put them in the East corners of their rooms. They will henceforth light lamps and candles before these pictures. The candle before the picture is, as we know, man's life being lived in front of the vision of Jerusalem; man's ordinary daily life in the presence of the heavenly city.

We realise life itself as the pilgrimage of pilgrimages. Life contains many pilgrimages to Jerusalem, just as it contains many flowerings of spring to summer, just as it contains many feasts of Communion and not merely one. Some of the pilgrims actually go as many as ten times to that Jerusalem in Palestine. But there are Jerusalems in other places if they only knew, and pilgrimages in other modes. It is possible to go back and live the pilgrimage in another way, and to find another Jerusalem. Life has its depths: we will go down into them. We may forget the vision there, but as a true pilgrim once said, "We shall always live again to see our golden hour of victory." That is the true pilgrim's faith. He will reach Jerusalem again and again. He may forget, but he will always remember again; he will always rise again to the light of memory. Deep in the depths of this dark universe our little daily sun is shining, but up above there is another Sun. At times throughout our life we rise to the surface, and for a minute catch a glimpse of that Sun's light: at each of these times we shall have attained unto Jerusalem and have completed a pilgrimage within the pilgrimage. There is light on the faces of those living heroically: it is the light of the vision of Jerusalem.

VII

THE MESSAGE FROM THE HERMIT

THE question remains, "Who is the tramp?" Who is the walking person seen from the vantage ground of these pages? He is necessarily a masked figure; he wears the disguise of one who has escaped, and also of one who is a conspirator. He is not the dilettante literary person gone tramping, nor the pauper vagabond who writes sonnets, though either of these rôles may be part of his disguise. He is not merely something negligible or accidental or ornamental, he is something real and true, the product of his time, at once a phenomenon and a portent.

He is the walking hermit, the world-forsaker, but he is above all things a rebel and a prophet, and he stands in very distinct relation to the life of his time.

The great fact of the human world to-day is the tremendous commercial machine which is grinding out at a marvellous acceleration the smaller and meaner sort of man, the middle class, the average man, "the damned, compact, liberal majority," to use the words of Ibsen, and the world daily becomes "more **Chinese.**" The rocks are fraying one another down to desert sand, and mankind becomes a new Sahara.

But over and against the commercial machine stand the rebels, the defiers of it, those who wish to limit its power, to redeem some of the slaves, and to rebuild the temples which it has broken down.

Commercialism is at present the great enemy of the individual man. One already reads in leading articles such phrases as "our commercial, national, and imperial welfare"—commercial first, national second, imperial third, and spiritual nowhere.

Commercialism has already subdued the Church of Christ in Western Europe, it has disorganised the forces of art, and it tends to deny the living sources of religion, art, and life.

It remains for the rebel to assert that even though the name and idea of Christianity be sold—as was its Founder—for silver, though it be rendered an impotent and useless word, yet there is in mankind a religion which is independent of all names and all words, a spring of living water that may be subterraneanised for a while, but can never be altogether dammed and stopped; that there is an art which shall blossom through all ages, either in the secret places of the world or in the open, in the place of honour, as long as man lives upon the world.

And he does more than assert, than merely wind upon his horn outside the gates of the enchanted city, he is a builder, collector, saver. He wishes to find the few who, in this fearful commercial submersion, ought to be living the spiritual life, and showing forth in blossom the highest significance of the Adam tree. He himself lives the life which more must of necessity live, if only as a matter of salt to save the body politic.

It has been urged, "You are unpracticable; you want a world of tramps—how are you going to live?" But we no more want a world of tramps than the promiser of new life wants a world of promisers: we want a world that will take the life promised.

As I have said, we want first of all the few, the hermits, saints, the altogether lovely men and women, the blossoming of the race. It is necessary that these be found or that they find themselves, and that they take their true orbits and live their true lives; for all the rest of ordinary humanity is waiting to live its life in relation to these. The few must live their lives out to the full in order that all others may live their lives completely; for the temple of humanity has not only the broad floor, but the Cross glittering above the pinnacle.

The night is dark, but there is plenty of hope for the future; the very extremity of our calamity is something that bids us hope. Fifty years ago nobody would listen to a gospel of rebellion, and such a great man as Carlyle was actually preaching that to labour is to pray. To-day men are ready to lay down their working tools and listen to any insurrectionist, so aware has mankind become of an impending spiritual bankruptcy. Never in any preceding generation has the young man standing on the threshold of life felt more unsettled. His unsettlement has frequently turned to frenzy and anarchy in individual cases. Never has he cast his eyes about more desperately for a way of redemption or a spiritual leader. For him, as for all of us, the one requirement is to find out what is the *first* thing to do; not the nearest, but the *first,* the most essential; the one after which all other things naturally take their places.

It is not to wreck the great machine, for that would be to rush to the other extreme of ruin and disorder. It is not even, as I think, to build a new machine, for that would be to enter into a wasteful competition wherein we should spend without profit and with much loss of brotherly love, all our patience and our new desires.

The one way and the first way is to use and subordinate the present machine, to limit it to its true domain, and let it be our true and vital servant.

But how?

By finding the few who can live the life of communion, the few who can show forth the true significance of the race. By saving our most precious thoughts and ideals, and adding them to the similar thoughts and ideals of others, by putting the instruments of education in their proper places, by separating and saving in the world of literature and art the expressions of beauty which are valuable to the coming race, as distinguished from those that are merely sold for a price. By the making solitary, which is making sacred.

For instance, I would have the famous and wonderful pictures now foiling and dwarfing one another in our vulgar galleries, distributed over the Western world. I wish their enfranchisement. Each great picture should be given a room to itself, like the Sistine Madonna, not only a room but a temple like that of the Iverskaya at Moscow, not only a temple but a fair populous province. The great pictures should be objects of pilgrimages, and their temples places of prayer. In the galleries, as is obvious, the pictures are at their smallest, their glory pressed back into themselves or overlapped or smudged by the confusing glory of others. Out in the wide world, enshrined in temples, these pictures would become living hearts, they would have arms dealing out blessings, they would outgrow again till their influence was as wide as the little kingdoms in which they were enshrined. Pictures would again work miracles. What is more, great pictures would again be painted.

This illustration is valuable allegorically. Great pictures are very like great souls, very like great and beautiful ideas. What is true for pictures is true for men.

The men who feel in themselves the instinct for the new life must take steps to make space for themselves and to make temples. Where they find the beautiful, the real, they must take it to themselves and protect it from enemies, they must at once begin to build walls of defence. So great is their responsibility and so delicate their charge that they must challenge no one, and invite no discussion and no hostility. They must have and hold their own beautiful life as they would a fair young bride.

Where they have visions they must build temples, as the Russian mouzhiks build churches and put up crosses. Of course I do not mean material temples, but temples not made by hands, temples of spirit, temples of remembrance. Where they read in books sacred pages they must make these pages sacred, sacred for them. Where they find men noble they must have reference to the noble part of them and deny the other. They have to win back the beautiful churches and cathedrals. Often it is said nowadays, "Such and such a church is wonderful and its service lifts one to heaven, but the clergyman and his sermon are impossible." But though a clergyman can condition his congregation it is much more true that the congregation can condition the clergyman. It is written, "Where two or three are gathered together in My Name, there am I in the midst of them." When they in the pews are those in white robes, then He in the pulpit is the Christ Himself.

In literature we have to differentiate what is purely a commercial product like the yellow-back novel, what is educational like the classic, and what is of the new. With the commercial we have of course no traffic; the classic is a place for those still learning what has already been said, a place for orientisation, for finding out where one stands. In this category are the Shakespearean performances at the theatre. In any case the classic is necessarily subordinate to the new literature, the literature of pioneering and discovery, the literature of ourselves. It is the school which prepares for the stepping forth on the untrodden ways.

This fencing off, differentiation and allocation, these defences of the beautiful and new, and of the temples enshrining them, shall be like the walls round a new sanctuary. We shall thereby protect ourselves from the encroaching commercial machine, its dwarfing ethics, mean postulates, and accurst conventions, and we shall rear within the walls all the beautiful that the outside world says does not exist. We shall find a whole new world of those who despise the honours and prizes of the commercial machine, and who care not for the shows, diversions, pleasures, and gambles provided for commercial slaves. But it will not cause those of that world to falter if the great multitude of their fellow-men scoff at them or think that they miss life.

Our work is then to separate off and consecrate the beautiful, to bring the beautiful together and organise it, not renouncing the machine, but only taking from it the service necessary for our physical needs, in no case being ruled or guided by it or its exigencies. When we have accomplished that, a miracle is promised. The outside world will take shape against our walls and receive its life through our gates—it will come into relation to us even to the ends of the earth. The new heart means the salvation of all.

With that we necessarily return to ourselves, the out-flung units of modern life, tramps so called, rebels, hermits, the portents of the new era, the first signs of spring after dark winter; some of us, the purely lyrical, spring flowers; others the prophetic and dynamic, spring winds—who blowing, shall blow upon winter, as Nietzsche says, "with a thawing wind."

We are many: I speak for thousands who are voiceless. But we are feeble, for we know not one another: we shall know.

A new summer is coming and a new adventure; and summer, as all know, is the year itself, the other seasons being purely subordinate. We are as yet but February heralds. Nevertheless we ask, standing without the gates of the sleeping city of winter, "Who of ye within the city are stepping forth unto the new adventure?" Strange powers are to them; the mysterious spells of the earth, the renewal of inspiration at the life source, the essence of new summer colours, the idea of new summer shapes. To the young men and women of to-day there is a chance to be as beautiful as it is possible to be upon this little earth, a chance to find all the significance of life and beauty that is possible for man to know, a chance to be of the same substance as the fire of stars, a chance of perfection. It is the voice of the hermit crying from the wilderness: "I have come back from God with a message and a blessing—come out ye young men and maidens, for a new season is at hand."

THE END

The Codes Of Hammurabi And Moses
W. W. Davies

QTY

The discovery of the Hammurabi Code is one of the greatest achievements of archaeology, and is of paramount interest, not only to the student of the Bible, but also to all those interested in ancient history...

Religion   **ISBN:** *1-59462-338-4*

Pages:132
MSRP $12.95

The Theory of Moral Sentiments
Adam Smith

QTY

This work from 1749. contains original theories of conscience amd moral judgment and it is the foundation for systemof morals.

Philosophy **ISBN:** *1-59462-777-0*

Pages:536
MSRP $19.95

Jessica's First Prayer
Hesba Stretton

QTY

In a screened and secluded corner of one of the many railway-bridges which span the streets of London there could be seen a few years ago, from five o'clock every morning until half past eight, a tidily set-out coffee-stall, consisting of a trestle and board, upon which stood two large tin cans, with a small fire of charcoal burning under each so as to keep the coffee boiling during the early hours of the morning when the work-people were thronging into the city on their way to their daily toil...

Pages:84

Childrens   **ISBN:** *1-59462-373-2*

MSRP $9.95

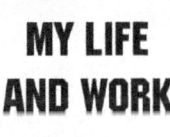

My Life and Work
Henry Ford

QTY

Henry Ford revolutionized the world with his implementation of mass production for the Model T automobile. Gain valuable business insight into his life and work with his own auto-biography... "We have only started on our development of our country we have not as yet, with all our talk of wonderful progress, done more than scratch the surface. The progress has been wonderful enough but..."

Pages:300

Biographies/   **ISBN:** *1-59462-198-5*

MSRP $21.95

The Art of Cross-Examination
Francis Wellman

QTY

I presume it is the experience of every author, after his first book is published upon an important subject, to be almost overwhelmed with a wealth of ideas and illustrations which could readily have been included in his book, and which to his own mind, at least, seem to make a second edition inevitable. Such certainly was the case with me; and when the first edition had reached its sixth impression in five months, I rejoiced to learn that it seemed to my publishers that the book had met with a sufficiently favorable reception to justify a second and considerably enlarged edition. ...

Pages:412

Reference   ISBN: *1-59462-647-2*   *MSRP $19.95*

On the Duty of Civil Disobedience
Henry David Thoreau

QTY

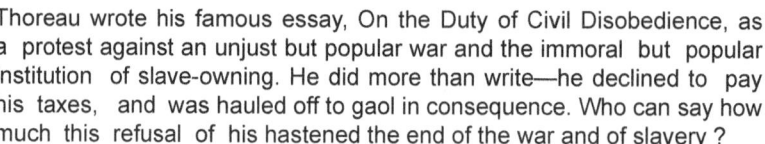

Thoreau wrote his famous essay, On the Duty of Civil Disobedience, as a protest against an unjust but popular war and the immoral but popular institution of slave-owning. He did more than write—he declined to pay his taxes, and was hauled off to gaol in consequence. Who can say how much this refusal of his hastened the end of the war and of slavery ?

Law   ISBN: *1-59462-747-9*   **Pages:48**

MSRP $7.45

Dream Psychology Psychoanalysis for Beginners
Sigmund Freud

QTY

Sigmund Freud, born Sigismund Schlomo Freud (May 6, 1856 - September 23, 1939), was a Jewish-Austrian neurologist and psychiatrist who co-founded the psychoanalytic school of psychology. Freud is best known for his theories of the unconscious mind, especially involving the mechanism of repression; his redefinition of sexual desire as mobile and directed towards a wide variety of objects; and his therapeutic techniques, especially his understanding of transference in the therapeutic relationship and the presumed value of dreams as sources of insight into unconscious desires.

Dream Psychology
Psychoanalysis for Beginners

Sigmund Freud

Pages:196

Psychology   ISBN: *1-59462-905-6*   *MSRP $15.45*

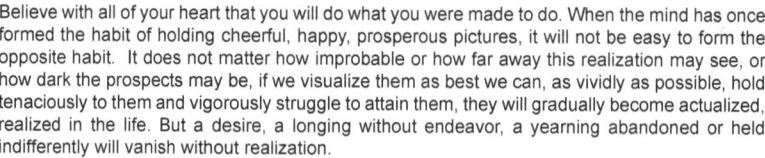

The Miracle of Right Thought
Orison Swett Marden

QTY

Believe with all of your heart that you will do what you were made to do. When the mind has once formed the habit of holding cheerful, happy, prosperous pictures, it will not be easy to form the opposite habit. It does not matter how improbable or how far away this realization may see, or how dark the prospects may be, if we visualize them as best we can, as vividly as possible, hold tenaciously to them and vigorously struggle to attain them, they will gradually become actualized, realized in the life. But a desire, a longing without endeavor, a yearning abandoned or held indifferently will vanish without realization.

Pages:360

Self Help   ISBN: *1-59462-644-8*   *MSRP $25.45*

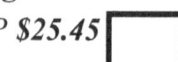

www.bookjungle.com *email: sales@bookjungle.com fax: 630-214-0564 mail: Book Jungle PO Box 2226 Champaign, IL 61825*

QTY

The Rosicrucian Cosmo-Conception Mystic Christianity *by Max Heindel* ISBN: *1-59462-188-8* **$38.95**
The Rosicrucian Cosmo-conception is not dogmatic, neither does it appeal to any other authority than the reason of the student. It is: not controversial, but is: sent forth in the, hope that it may help to clear... *New Age/Religion Pages 646*

Abandonment To Divine Providence *by Jean-Pierre de Caussade* ISBN: *1-59462-228-0* **$25.95**
"The Rev. Jean Pierre de Caussade was one of the most remarkable spiritual writers of the Society of Jesus in France in the 18th Century. His death took place at Toulouse in 1751. His works have gone through many editions and have been republished... *Inspirational/Religion Pages 400*

Mental Chemistry *by Charles Haanel* ISBN: *1-59462-192-6* **$23.95**
Mental Chemistry allows the change of material conditions by combining and appropriately utilizing the power of the mind. Much like applied chemistry creates something new and unique out of careful combinations of chemicals the mastery of mental chemistry... *New Age Pages 354*

The Letters of Robert Browning and Elizabeth Barret Barrett 1845-1846 vol II ISBN: *1-59462-193-4* **$35.95**
by Robert Browning and Elizabeth Barrett *Biographies Pages 596*

Gleanings In Genesis (volume I) *by Arthur W. Pink* ISBN: *1-59462-130-6* **$27.45**
Appropriately has Genesis been termed "the seed plot of the Bible" for in it we have, in germ form, almost all of the great doctrines which are afterwards fully developed in the books of Scripture which follow... *Religion/Inspirational Pages 420*

The Master Key *by L. W. de Laurence* ISBN: *1-59462-001-6* **$30.95**
In no branch of human knowledge has there been a more lively increase of the spirit of research during the past few years than in the study of Psychology, Concentration and Mental Discipline. The requests for authentic lessons in Thought Control, Mental Discipline and... *New Age/Business Pages 422*

The Lesser Key Of Solomon Goetia *by L. W. de Laurence* ISBN: *1-59462-092-X* **$9.95**
This translation of the first book of the "Lernegton" which is now for the first time made accessible to students of Talismanic Magic was done, after careful collation and edition, from numerous Ancient Manuscripts in Hebrew, Latin, and French... *New Age/Occult Pages 92*

Rubaiyat Of Omar Khayyam *by Edward Fitzgerald* ISBN:*1-59462-332-5* **$13.95**
Edward Fitzgerald, whom the world has already learned, in spite of his own efforts to remain within the shadow of anonymity, to look upon as one of the rarest poets of the century, was born at Bredfield, in Suffolk, on the 31st of March, 1809. He was the third son of John Purcell... *Music Pages 172*

Ancient Law *by Henry Maine* ISBN: *1-59462-128-4* **$29.95**
The chief object of the following pages is to indicate some of the earliest ideas of mankind, as they are reflected in Ancient Law, and to point out the relation of those ideas to modern thought. *Religion/History Pages 452*

Far-Away Stories *by William J. Locke* ISBN: *1-59462-129-2* **$19.45**
"Good wine needs no bush, but a collection of mixed vintages does. And this book is just such a collection. Some of the stories I do not want to remain buried for ever in the museum files of dead magazine-numbers an author's not unpardonable vanity..." *Fiction Pages 272*

Life of David Crockett *by David Crockett* ISBN: *1-59462-250-7* **$27.45**
"Colonel David Crockett was one of the most remarkable men of the times in which he lived. Born in humble life, but gifted with a strong will, an indomitable courage, and unremitting perseverance... *Biographies/New Age Pages 424*

Lip-Reading *by Edward Nitchie* ISBN: *1-59462-206-X* **$25.95**
Edward B. Nitchie, founder of the New York School for the Hard of Hearing, now the Nitchie School of Lip-Reading, Inc, wrote "LIP-READING Principles and Practice". The development and perfecting of this meritorious work on lip-reading was an undertaking... *How-to Pages 400*

A Handbook of Suggestive Therapeutics, Applied Hypnotism, Psychic Science ISBN: *1-59462-214-0* **$24.95**
by Henry Munro *Health/New Age/Health/Self-help Pages 376*

A Doll's House: and Two Other Plays *by Henrik Ibsen* ISBN: *1-59462-112-8* **$19.95**
Henrik Ibsen created this classic when in revolutionary 1848 Rome. Introducing some striking concepts in playwriting for the realist genre, this play has been studied the world over. *Fiction/Classics/Plays 308*

The Light of Asia *by sir Edwin Arnold* ISBN: *1-59462-204-3* **$13.95**
In this poetic masterpiece, Edwin Arnold describes the life and teachings of Buddha. The man who was to become known as Buddha to the world was born as Prince Gautama of India but he rejected the worldly riches and abandoned the reigns of power when... *Religion/History/Biographies Pages 170*

The Complete Works of Guy de Maupassant *by Guy de Maupassant* ISBN: *1-59462-157-8* **$16.95**
"For days and days, nights and nights, I had dreamed of that first kiss which was to consecrate our engagement, and I knew not on what spot I should put my lips..." *Fiction/Classics Pages 240*

The Art of Cross-Examination *by Francis L. Wellman* ISBN: *1-59462-309-0* **$26.95**
Written by a renowned trial lawyer, Wellman imparts his experience and uses case studies to explain how to use psychology to extract desired information through questioning. *How-to/Science/Reference Pages 408*

Answered or Unanswered? *by Louisa Vaughan* ISBN: *1-59462-248-5* **$10.95**
Miracles of Faith in China *Religion Pages 112*

The Edinburgh Lectures on Mental Science (1909) *by Thomas* ISBN: *1-59462-008-3* **$11.95**
This book contains the substance of a course of lectures recently given by the writer in the Queen Street Hall, Edinburgh. Its purpose is to indicate the Natural Principles governing the relation between Mental Action and Material Conditions... *New Age/Psychology Pages 148*

Ayesha *by H. Rider Haggard* ISBN: *1-59462-301-5* **$24.95**
Verily and indeed it is the unexpected that happens! Probably if there was one person upon the earth from whom the Editor of this, and of a certain previous history, did not expect to hear again... *Classics Pages 380*

Ayala's Angel *by Anthony Trollope* ISBN: *1-59462-352-X* **$29.95**
The two girls were both pretty, but Lucy who was twenty-one who supposed to be simple and comparatively unattractive, whereas Ayala was credited, as her Bombwhat romantic name might show, with poetic charm and a taste for romance. Ayala when her father died was nineteen... *Fiction Pages 484*

The American Commonwealth *by James Bryce* ISBN: *1-59462-286-8* **$34.45**
An interpretation of American democratic political theory. It examines political mechanics and society from the perspective of Scotsman James Bryce *Politics Pages 572*

Stories of the Pilgrims *by Margaret P. Pumphrey* ISBN: *1-59462-116-0* **$17.95**
This book explores pilgrims religious oppression in England as well as their escape to Holland and eventual crossing to America on the Mayflower, and their early days in New England... *History Pages 268*

QTY

The Fasting Cure *by Sinclair Upton* ISBN: *1-59462-222-1* **$13.95**
In the Cosmopolitan Magazine for May, 1910, and in the Contemporary Review (London) for April, 1910, I published an article dealing with my experiences in fasting. I have written a great many magazine articles, but never one which attracted so much attention... New Age/Self Help/Health Pages 164

Hebrew Astrology *by Sepharial* ISBN: *1-59462-308-2* **$13.45**
In these days of advanced thinking it is a matter of common observation that we have left many of the old landmarks behind and that we are now pressing forward to greater heights and to a wider horizon than that which represented the mind-content of our progenitors... Astrology Pages 144

Thought Vibration or The Law of Attraction in the Thought World ISBN: *1-59462-127-6* **$12.95**
by William Walker Atkinson Psychology/Religion Pages 144

Optimism *by Helen Keller* ISBN: *1-59462-108-X* **$15.95**
Helen Keller was blind, deaf, and mute since 19 months old, yet famously learned how to overcome these handicaps, communicate with the world, and spread her lectures promoting optimism. An inspiring read for everyone... Biographies/Inspirational Pages 84

Sara Crewe *by Frances Burnett* ISBN: *1-59462-360-0* **$9.45**
In the first place, Miss Minchin lived in London. Her home was a large, dull, tall one, in a large, dull square, where all the houses were alike, and all the sparrows were alike, and where all the door-knockers made the same heavy sound... Childrens/Classic Pages 88

The Autobiography of Benjamin Franklin *by Benjamin Franklin* ISBN: *1-59462-135-7* **$24.95**
The Autobiography of Benjamin Franklin has probably been more extensively read than any other American historical work, and no other book of its kind has had such ups and downs of fortune. Franklin lived for many years in England, where he was agent... Biographies/History Pages 332

Name	
Email	
Telephone	
Address	
City, State ZIP	

☐ **Credit Card**   ☐ **Check / Money Order**

Credit Card Number	
Expiration Date	
Signature	

Please Mail to: Book Jungle
PO Box 2226
Champaign, IL 61825
or Fax to: 630-214-0564

ORDERING INFORMATION

web: *www.bookjungle.com*
email: *sales@bookjungle.com*
fax: *630-214-0564*
mail: *Book Jungle PO Box 2226 Champaign, IL 61825*
or PayPal *to sales@bookjungle.com*

Please contact us for bulk discounts

DIRECT-ORDER TERMS

**20% Discount if You Order
Two or More Books**
Free Domestic Shipping!
Accepted: Master Card, Visa,
Discover, American Express

www.ingramcontent.com/pod-product-compliance
Lightning Source LLC
Chambersburg PA
CBHW080907020726
47502CB00008B/2373